HIGH
TO SHAME

Geoff Malcolm

Safe Sex is essential: your very life may depend on it. Please remember that some of the sexual practices that are featured in this work of fiction (about an era that pre-dates lethal STDs) are dangerous and they are not recommended or in any way endorsed by the publishers; by the same token, we do not condone any form of non-consensual sex for any reason: it is reprehensible and illegal and should never become a part of a person's real life: rather it should remain firmly in the realm of sexual fantasy.

Highway to Shame
Past Venus Press
London 2009

Past Venus Press
is an imprint of
Erotic Review Books

ERB, 31 Sinclair Road,
LONDON W14 0NS
Tel: +44 (0) 207 371 1532
Email: enquiries@eroticprints.org
Web: www.eroticprints.org
© 2009 MacHo Ltd, London UK

Illustrations by Tom Sargent

ISBN : 9781904989622

Printed and bound in the UK by Cox & Wyman Ltd

No part of this publication may be reproduced by any means without the express written permission of the Publishers. The moral right of the author of the text and the artist has been asserted.

While every effort has been made by PVP to contact copyright holders it may not have been possible to get in touch with certain publishers or authors of former editions of some of the titles published in this series.

Highway To Shame

Geoff Malcolm

CHAPTER ONE

When he looked into the rear-view mirror of the pickup camper he was driving, Dave Christie could see a cluster of four motorcycles following him up the long grade. Two or three times the lead motorcyclist had tried to pass him, but the twisting, narrow road, the stream of approaching traffic and Dave's reluctance to pull into one of the turnouts, had prevented them from passing his labouring truck. He listened, critically, to the engine and swore under his breath. There were a couple of fouled spark plugs, which caused the motor to run roughly, reducing its power and his speed. Then, he saw that behind the motorcycles there was a growing tail of other vehicles, including another camper and a couple of cars pulling light vacation trailers. He'd have to pull over pretty soon to allow them to pass, but there were no turnouts along this stretch of the road.

This was the third day of his vacation. He'd been looking forward to it for months, but so far there had been nothing but trouble. On their first day away from home a radiator hose had broken, which delayed them for two hours for repairs; as a result they had been forced to stay overnight in a commercial trailer camp. Yesterday, he'd replaced the water pump... and now, today, it was fouled spark plugs.

A frown spread across his handsomely rugged face, and his deep, brown eyes glowered behind his heavy, black-rimmed glasses at the images in the rear-view mirror then studied the road ahead for space to pull over. The heavily loaded truck ground slowly up the steep grade in second gear, the punished engine whining its protest. Angrily, Dave stomped down hard on the already fully opened accelerator and growled, "Come on... let's go... God damn it!"

Sitting beside her husband, Lauren Christie studied his profile through wide, clear blue eyes. She knew he was angry. The first two days of their holiday hadn't been very pleasant. The extra expense and the delays for repairs had made him increasingly exasperated. Her knowledge of machines was limited, but even to her unpracticed ear, the sounds of the labouring engine told her there was something wrong.

"What seems to be wrong with the motor, Dave?" she asked, finally, breaking a long, silence.

"Couple of dirty spark plugs!" He didn't turn his head to answer her question.

She, also, could see the long string of motorcycles, cars and campers behind them. Since their camper was the first in the line, it was their vehicle that was holding back the traffic.

"Shouldn't we pull over... and let those other people pass us?"

Dave snapped back, "Sure! Hell yes... I should... but there are no turn-outs!"

"You passed a couple of them... back there..."

"You want to drive this rig?" he shot back.

"No... but..."

"Then... shut up... and get the hell off my back!"

For perhaps the thousandth time, it seemed to Lauren, she turned silently away, her deep blue eyes brimming with tears. Their vacation, too, was turning sour... just as everything about their marriage seemed to be falling apart. She had promised herself that these two weeks away from the cares of day-to-day living and home-making chores would be happy ones; days that would heal some of the wounds, solve some of their differences... and draw them closer together... perhaps, even, regenerate their feelings of tenderness for each other... and rejuvenate the sexual side of their lives. She sighed with self-pity and a nostalgic longing for things as they had been... when they were first married; of course, even then there had been some problems, but she and Dave had been younger then. They had been full of hope and optimism, but now... She dabbed at her eyes with a tissue and turned to look out at the mountain landscape, the forested slopes which offered a serenity she didn't feel.

The sudden roar of a motor close beside the camper caused her to look back quickly, with startled eyes, at the lead motorcyclist, who had then drawn abreast of the cab. She saw a black beard, long black hair whipping in the wind, a pair of dark eyes flashing, angrily, and an open mouth that roared, obscenely, the words partially snatched away by the wind.

"of-a-bitch! Get... fucking... off the road!"

With a roar, the motorcycle swept by them. A second figure, smaller and definitely feminine, clung behind the driver. She, too, was shouting, although it was difficult to understand what she was saying.

A straight stretch of road lay ahead of them for about seventy-five yards, devoid of approaching cars, which was the reason the group of four motorcyclists chose to pass, right then. As the leader swept by, he shook a threatening fist, then flipped his middle finger up in the age-old signal of insult. Lauren's sensibilities were injured. The auburn-haired, pixie-faced girl, on the back of the motorcycle, looked back at them and made the self-same sign.

Then, in quick succession, the other three

motorcyclists thundered by the slow-moving camper, each hooting a string of obscenities and following the example of the leader, flipped the lewd finger at Dave and Lauren.

Dave's temper boiled over, instantly, and he was shouting back, "Well... fuck you, too... you bastards!"

"Please... Dave... do you have to be like them?" Lauren chided. She didn't like to hear him use those words. It always seemed so unnecessary, so vulgar.

"Goddamn it!" he flared back at her. "I'll say what I like... and right now I'm good and mad! Plug your ears up... if you don't want to hear it!"

The fourth and last cyclist had just passed him, when a low-slung sports car came snarling around a curve toward them. Lauren was sure there would be a collision, but the motorcycle rider ducked to his side of the road, at the last instant, with only inches to spare.

"Why... you stupid bastard!" Dave roared, visibly shaken by the close call... the possibility of being involved in the smash-up, had the sports car and the motorcycle crashed together.

Just around the next curve, a highway sign warned of a turnout ahead, and Dave heaved a sigh of relief, as he studied the rear-view mirror, again, to see that there were ten or more cars strung out behind his camper. He pulled off the road into the cleared space, trying to ignore the grim faces of the drivers who swept by on the road. Some of the people were outright angry. He could see their mouths move, cursing him, insultingly... But, Christ! He rationalized. I can't help it if the damned engine's acting up!

He consulted a California highway map. "There's a little town up ahead... maybe fifteen miles or so..." he observed. "I can get a set of new spark plugs there... then it's only about sixty miles to that State Park..."

Lauren wasn't really listening. She agreed, absently, "That's good..." then added, "maybe... we can get to bed earlier, tonight... and..."

"Yeah and get a good night's sleep, for a change so we can get on the road earlier..."

"I wasn't thinking... just about sleep..." Lauren murmured, a faint smile playing on her lips, her eyebrows raised in mild suggestion.

"Oh, you mean something else, like sex? Well it's according to how tired I am. Okay?"

"I guess it'll have to be... all right..." she sighed with resignation, hoping against hope that he wouldn't be too tired, too busy... too drunk... or too something. It seemed, lately, that was the story of their married sex-life. She decided to change the subject.

"Did you notice what that girl... on the back of the motorcycle did?"

"No... what did she do?" Dave responded, looking back down the road to see that the traffic had cleared. He put the truck in gear and eased out onto the narrow highway.

"She made that offensive sign... with her hand, too!"

"Oh, that! Just consider the source! They're just a bunch of worthless motorcycle bums! They probably belong to one of those clubs or gangs!"

"She seemed to be the only girl... and there were four men..."

"I wouldn't know!" He dismissed the subject. "Who can tell the difference... with their long hair?"

"The difference... is the shape..."

Dave was listening to the truck's motor. It was running even more roughly, as it groaned and whined up the long grade.

"I hope we can make it to that little town, now!" he grunted. "We've got to get this damned thing running better!"

***

Settling down into his sleeping bag, luxuriously, and scratching his long, lean and muscular flanks, Hunter Mitchell was thoughtful. He was thinking about that luscious blonde he had first spotted in the service station, yesterday. She was waiting around there while something was being fixed on their camper... of course, she was straight, and her husband was a typical nine-to-five establishment type, full of apple pie, mother and patriotism crap. Kerr-rist I can spot those mothahs a mile away!

But, that woman of his! Man... the way she was flipping her ass around in those tight hot pants... and those tits, and those legs that wouldn't stop! She was something else! Damn, I'd like to get into a mama like that... for some plain and fancy fucking!

Down between his legs, his scrotum tightened up and began to lift his balls, gradually, up tight to his crotch; at the same time, the shaft of his cock swelled with hot blood. It began to throb to full erection, and his hand went down to grasp the growing massiveness of it. He conceded to himself that the little blonde bitch wasn't available to him, so he'd just have to make do with what was handy... and what was always there, of course, was Billie. She was there... any time he wanted a piece of ass... And, she'd better be here!

***

One unbreakable rule was that his mama, pixie-faced Billie Grant, had to be around... whenever he wanted her... for whatever reason! And, Hunter wanted her, now!

He threw back the top portion of the unzipped, double sleeping bag and called, softly, "Billie!"

There was no answer. The black-bearded leader waited a beat or to, before he called, again, louder, *"Billlieee!"*

On the heavily wooded slope above the camp, Billie heard Hunter's voice calling her, the second time. She froze. She had to obey him... no matter what! But please! Not right now, though!

She was crouched over Dipstick MacKay's loins, his long, thin cock held in her hands, her lips just beginning to descend on it to engulf his cock's head in her hungry mouth.

Hastily, she began to scramble to her feet, dropping the fully erect prick lancing up through the fly of his heavy, leather motorcycle pants.

"That's Hunter!" she gasped. "I've got to split!"

MacKay sat up, reached out and grabbed one of her wrists.

"Let him wait! You're mine... right now!" he hissed.

"No Dipstick! Christ no! I've got to go!" Her voice was desperate. "You know that!"

"Stop... calling... me... Dipstick... for fuck's sake! My name's Danny! Me and him are going to have a go about that one of these days!"

"Let me go!" Billie begged. "I don't want him to get pissed-off at me... over nothing!"

"Nothing!?" Danny MacKay roared. "You're splitting... leaving me all uptight, with a big hard-on, ready to do some serious fucking... you call that nothing?"

"But... I've got to go! I don't want Hunter... carving on me... the way he did Annie!" She wrenched herself free of his grasp, a dry sob escaping her contorted mouth. As she started down the slope toward the camp, Billie flung back over her shoulder, "You can jerk it off... or find out, for sure, whether Superboy wants to blow you!"

Then, she heard Hunter call for the third time. His voice was loud, angry, "Billie! Get your fucking ass over here... right now!"

Terror-stricken, she called out, "I'm coming! I'm coming!" *God! He had to call me three times!*

She ran... hard, barely able to see in the darkness, stumbling once or twice and cursing her rotten luck. The fright in her was real. Hunter demanded absolute obedience of his mamas, and any breaches of his iron discipline were dealt with, instantly... harshly.

Arriving out of breath at his sleeping bag, where Hunter sat glowering, angrily, Billie flung herself down on her knees before him, her petite, gamine features distraught, her scared blue eyes already pleading for a mercy she knew he wouldn't dispense. She brushed disheveled strands of lustrous auburn hair away from her face and trembled, "Here I... am... Hunter!"

"Where the hell you been?"

"Up there... on the hill... but I-I... didn't hear you!" she defended, hoping he would soften... perhaps allow her this one trespass against his rigid rules.

"Who was up there with you?"

"Dipstick..." she admitted, truthfully, knowing that she could not tell Hunter any more than that. God! I-I can't tell him Dipstick wouldn't let me go! She didn't want to be the cause of an open rift between the two men; there was already enough animosity between them.

"Dipstick? Christ!" The black-bearded leader was silent for a moment. Danny 'Dipstick' MacKay needed to learn a few things. There wasn't any doubt about it, but he'd have to take care of MacKay, tomorrow. Right now, his mama would get her little lesson in obedience before he fucked her.

"All right... get those God damned rags off! I want you bare-assed naked!"

Hunter watched her, avidly, his eyes burning with lewd desire and a grim satisfaction, as she hastened to obey him.

Sitting back on the sleeping bag, she pulled off her heavy boots and thick socks, then standing up, she unbuckled the wide belt, opened the fly of her boys' jeans and stripped them down over the soft, white columns of her tapering thighs and the long, svelte curve of her calves. Next, she removed her heavy, leather jacket, and with trembling fingers, unbuttoned her man's shirt, tossing it aside with her other articles of clothing. She wore nothing under it. Her breasts soared free in the wash of the cool evening air, standing out in luscious, globular mounds, slightly upthrust and glowing in alabaster whiteness, each of them crowned with the rosy pink of nipples already spiking out into cones of erectile arousal. They were young, tender breasts, firm and high on her chest, the valley between them deep and clearly defined. Then, without hesitation, she slipped her panties down over the curving swell of her hips and buttocks to stand completely nude before him.

His massive, long and thick cock throbbed with anticipation, as he watched. Damn! She was the most luscious mama he'd ever had! He almost hated to have to discipline her... But, hell... you let a mama get away with one little thing... and there's no end to the crap they'll try to pull on you!

"Now... give me your belt!" he ordered.

"P-Please... Hunter..." she pleaded, her lower lip trembling, wide, blue eyes glistening with tears, "I-I really didn't hear... y-you..."

He wouldn't be swayed. "I said give me your goddamned belt... or do you want me to use mine?"

"Oh, no! God no!" Hastily, she stopped to pick up her discarded jeans and unthreaded the wide, leather belt from the loops, a vivid impression in her mind of what his studded belt would do to her flesh were he to use it! Abjectly, she handed the plain, leather strap to him.

"Down on your belly, bitch... and take your medicine!" Hunter commanded. "And... not one squeal... dig?"

"P-Please... don't... mark me..." she whispered. But Billie knew there was no escaping her punishment.

She had known from the beginning that he intended to carry it out. It's not fair! It wasn't my fault... but I'll have to take it!

"You disobeyed me!" Hunter grunted. "That's why you're getting it!" He doubled the belt and held it in one hand, while with the other, he snatched at her wrist and pulled her down onto the sleeping bag, then kneeling up, the black-bearded leader looked down at his target. As she lay there, Billie, undulated her hips, provocatively, the moons of her buttocks working, erotically... invitingly. It was a final ploy she used, almost unconsciously, in an attempt to dissuade him, but at the same time, she pushed her face down hard into the material of the sleeping bag, expecting, any second now, the slashing pain of the leather strap across her soft backside.

Hunter's big cock jerked, and his hand went down to stroke the hardened, throbbing shaft, as a thrill of sadistic pleasure keened through him. Damn! He was going to enjoy this! Somehow, it made the fucking... afterward, even more enjoyable, more intense. His lips peeled back in a lewd grin, his white teeth gleaming through the blackness of his beard. Suddenly, he raised his arm and brought the leather belt down hard and true in a solid, slashing blow across those lovely, white buttocks.

Crack!

Billie bit back her scream of pain. Her whole behind hurt. Oh, God! It burned like fire!

CRACK! His arm rose and fell for the second time, and Billie groaned aloud. She took a large mouthful of the material of the sleeping bag into her mouth. Never... never, would she cry out. It was part of the code she had to live by... as long as she rode with Hunter and his motorcycle gang. The almost unbearable pain seemed to spread out... down her twitching legs, up her back... and into her churning belly. God! Let me take it! I deserve it! Maybe... it's n-not f-fair but I did disobey... now, I've got to take my punishment...

For the third time, the belt in Hunter's hand slashed across her exposed buttocks. A muffled groan gurgled in her throat, and she knew that she would have screamed, full-throatedly, but for the cloth of the sleeping bag she had stuffed in her mouth. The searing pain was almost more than she could stand... but, now, unexplainably, there was something else. It was the warm glow of sexual arousal that began to pervade her loins. She was getting hot wanting it... wanting Hunter to fuck her and she didn't understand it.

Then, it was over. Her punishment was finished. Hunter tossed the belt onto the disordered pile of her clothing. "That's enough!" he snarled, reaching out to her and placing his hands on the smooth skin of her tiny waist.

Caressingly, his hands trailed downward over the rounded curves of her hips to the soft, resilient flesh of the lithe orbs of her just chastised buttocks. He could feel the cringing flesh, hot under his hands where the belt had struck... and there were the tiny ridges of raised welts. He grinned his lewdly sadistic satisfaction, as he went on, stroking and massaging the fully rounded protuberances of her bottom, and he was elated to feel her shiver, electrifyingly, her hips gyrating against the soft caresses he was now bestowing on her. Christ! It's going to flip me out... to fuck her, now!

"Well... Mama... that ought to be a lesson to you!" He stretched out on his back beside her.

Billie moaned something unintelligible, rolled to her side and crept into his arms, her firm, supple breasts flattening against the lean, hard muscles of his chest, and as she nuzzled into the hollow of his neck, she could smell the musky man-odor of his tanned, fit body. Her hand went down between them, immediately, to grasp with urgent meaning his long, thick and hardened cock. Gently, she pulled the heavy foreskin back, and her fingers lightly caressed his cock's head. It throbbed and jerked, vibrantly, in her hand.

Billie heard his grunt of pleasure, as her hand barely encircled the hot, pulsing shaft of his prick, her own passion already spiraling, the heated blood pounding in her loins, and she felt a wetness between her legs that told of her readiness, her growing desire.

Pressing her belly in tight to him, she parted her thighs, allowing her greedy little pussy to ride and buck up and down the hardness of his thigh muscle. Her lips, moist and slightly parted were offered up to him to be kissed.

His mouth, hot and wet crushed her own, and she felt his tongue burst into her oral vault to be sucked. Hungrily, she ovaled her lips to take it deep into her throat, while his hard, rough hands smoothed down over her back to the still painful flesh of her protruding buttocks to haul her up, tightly, to him. Her soft, resilient flesh didn't hurt as much now, but she could feel his hands so clearly... as though every square inch of her behind contained a million super-charged nerves. Meanwhile, her small hand was busy on the hard shaft of his cock, as she worked it up and down the massively solid length. His wiry beard and mustache tickled against her face, adding an extra erotic touch to her sexual arousal.

Hunter mumbled around her lips, "You're really hot for my cock, tonight... eh, Mama?"

"Oh, God... yes! I can't wait for you to... shove it in... and start fucking me!" she gasped, giving his prick a harder squeeze, as she milked at it, her upper leg going up over him to pull herself up even tighter to him. Now, she could feel the moisture that exuded from the head of his cock, the slippery, natural lubricant wetting the palm of her hand, and she rubbed it all around the bulbous head.

He was all she wanted, in this world. Oh, yes... it was true! Hunter was hard and tough... and he demanded strict obedience to his every whim; on the other hand, he protected her... took care of her. It was just like being married to him, except she could ball anyone else she pleased... just as long as she was there, when he wanted her. There were other aspects of their relationship she didn't like... such as his giving her to others to use... or inviting three or four at a time to fuck her every way there was in her book – and some that hadn't been written up, yet – but she was learning. He had never mentioned the word 'love'. She was sure he never would say it. Such an emotion was beyond him. Did Billie love the bearded gang leader? Perhaps... in her own way, she loved him, because she needed him and depended upon him. Would she ever leave him? Yes! That depended upon when he became tired of her... then she'd be replaced, completely... or she'd share him with another mama. If he shed himself of her... what then? She'd just have to find another rider. It was as simple as that! She didn't want to think about it. Right now, she was Hunter Mitchell's mama... and that was all that mattered!

Pulling her face back and away from him and breaking the deeply passionate kiss, she hissed, hoarsely, "Oh, God Hunter... I'm so ready... for you! Let's fuck... right now!"

She released his cock and rolled to her back to plant her widespread feet, solidly, her knees flexed and thighs splayed open, obscenely, as her hips ground in tiny circles under her, inviting his plundering entrance into her seething cunt.

"Well... I'm in the mood for a little cunt-lapping first!" he grunted. "You'll really pop, then!"

She watched him impatiently, as he rose to his knees with exasperating slowness and came between her spread legs, dropping his head down within bare inches above her warm, pulsing vaginal furrow. His long hair hung down to sweep across her naked loins, teasingly, and the tip of his bushy beard feathered down through the moist, pink flesh of her sensitive, yearning cunt. She shuddered with the delicious sensations being generated in her loins.

Excitedly, she begged him, then, "Oh, Hunter... Hunter... I don't care... whether you fuck it... or suck it... but p-please... *do something!*"

Hunter had never seen her this worked up, before... of course, he'd never fucked her this soon after administering a beating, either. He decided she must have liked it... that there was a masochistic streak in her, and he'd sure as hell remember it... in the future... Damn... that could lead to some real turned-on fucking!

He continued to smile with salacious satisfaction, as his eyes surveyed the feast she was offering him on the darkly auburn-haired platter of her delicate loins, the coral pink of her partially hidden slit sending shivers of anticipation keening along his spine. He noted where the delicious, narrow defile began at the bottom of her smooth, flat belly to slice downward, erotically, through the downy soft frizz of pubic hair to the full-rounded, alabaster orbs of her buttocks. She lifted her hips up, rotating them sensuously, expectantly, just inches from his bearded lips, and he heard an involuntary moan of frustrated anguish escape her lips.

"Oh! *Oooh...* God! Hunter! Don't do this... to me! Don't make me wait!"

With sadistically slow determination, he laid the palms of his hard hands high up on the soft, flesh of the insides of her quivering thighs, bracketing the narrow, pink slit, so that his thumbs could spread apart the velvety, yielding outer lips of her fleecy cunt. Then just as slowly, and with tantalizing purpose, he pulled open the slightly ragged coraline flanges of her pussy, until its bedewed, blushing portal lay exposed completely to his lustful eyes. Greedily, he ogled the breathtaking sight, wild spasms of passion jolting him, causing his cock to jerk and twitch, between his crouching legs.

He was entranced. He gaped down at the widespread opening that glistened dully in the dim light with viscous droplets of carnal desire. It seemed he could actually see it quiver and squirm, the intricate delicacies of her secret flesh begging his attentions.

Dropping his head down the last few inches, then, he plunged the full length of his long, agile tongue deep into the quivering, warm depths of her wildly clasping cunt. The truth was... he couldn't wait any longer, himself.

Billie had been beside herself, as she waited for what seemed interminably long moments. She was just going to begin begging him, abjectly, when she was rewarded with the exquisite sensation of his tongue thrusting deep into the heated moistness of her needful cuntal opening.

"OOOooohhh! Yeeeessssss! Oh, that's it! Suck me! Lick my pussy... good! Oh, it feels... so *goooooddd!"* she exulted, as she ground her loins up into his heavily bearded face with undulant eroticism, the need in her was urgent.

Then, Hunter felt her small hands clutching at his long, black hair, her fingers entwining large hands of it to haul his face, forcefully, into the splayed-but, moistly pink groove of her sensate cunt. She moaned and gasped almost incessantly, and he discerned the movements of her head flailing back and forth above, as he speared his hot tongue deep up into the warm, satiny depths of her dilating vagina.

Uncontrollably, Billie ground her hips down into the material of the sleeping bag, writhing and squirming with the ecstasy of her passion, little, unintelligible, animal-like mewlings come from between her clenched teeth, incessantly, then she would lift her loins up to him, pushing his face hard into the soft, golden curls of her pussy; at the same time, her fingers entangled in his hair pulled him in even tighter, as the sensitive, pulsating walls of her vagina seemed to open and close in a moist, sucking motion around the tantalizing thrustings of his tongue.

Exulting inwardly, the black-bearded leader grinned his satisfaction. His latest, tender, young mama was completely in his power. She was wild with desire... and getting wilder with each passing moment. He withdrew his agile, probing tongue and licked upward through the snug slit, pressuring through and parting the silky, auburn pubic hair, its tip flicking moistly in circles around the erect, swollen shaft of her clitoris, then his mouth engulfed all, his lips sucking and drawing the warm, soft folds of flesh into the hot cavern of his mouth, his tongue maintaining its maddening licking of the sensitive, pulsing bud of her womanhood.

"OOOooohhh... MY GOD!" she wailed, shudderingly, as the arcing sensations grounded on the head of her tender clitoris.

He raised his eyes to gaze sardonically at her beautifully contorted face. Her head still flailed back and forth, in tempo with his plundering tongue, as her fingers clutched tighter into his hair to direct his hungry, sucking mouth.

Looking up at her face through the valley of her breasts, his hands, suddenly, itched to caress and fondle, and they moved up over the snowy curve of her belly to the full, rounded firmness of her quivering, young breasts, his hard palms cupping, harshly, their velvet-skinned softness. His fingers rolled the rubbery hardness of her nipples, furiously, treating them cruelly, knowing that she preferred it that way. He chuckled to himself, as he heard her mewling moan of pleasure-pain. His newfound knowledge of her sexual arousal through pain gave him an extra sense of power over her. Hell! I can do anything I want to with her... and she'll love every fuckin' minute of it!

Suddenly, Billie felt him lifting her legs, and she knew a momentary disappointment, when his rough hands left her tingling breasts. With determined purpose, he folded her knees back until they pressed hard against her passion-swollen tits. His hands pushed on the backs of her knees, raising her wide-spread, flowered-open, naked cunt to expose her completely to his wild, probing tongue and hungrily sucking mouth... and it was then she felt the hot, moist contact of his tongue with her tight, puckered anal orifice, laving and probing, experimentally, at the sensitive, crinkled opening. It sent maddeningly tantalizing sensations of pure ecstasy surging through her trembling, lust-filled body. She moaned for pure joy, the anguished whine of rapture coming from deep in her chest. She had never experienced such irresistibly erotic pleasure. She had never known it could be so good. Briefly, her mind dwelt on and marveled at how it had begun for her... this time, the pain of the slashing belt across her backside turning her on to sex as she had never known it could exist... but she couldn't understand it... couldn't fathom how it had happened. She dismissed trying to understand, concentrating instead on the rapture of it.

Again, his tongue shot into the sensitive opening of her cunt, and she cried out, pleadingly, "Hunter! Oh, Hunter... use your big cock... now! Fuck me... in my cunt... with your hard cock! Please... Oh, please! I've got to have your cock... inside me... fucking me! Tear me apart with it! *Oooooooohhhhh!*"

Hunter Mitchell chortled his pleasure with her abject pleading to be fucked. That's the way he wanted it. He liked his mamas completely subjugated to his will.

"Okay!" he smiled, lewdly, up at her. "You're really turned on... aren't you?"

"Oh, God... I could climb walls... if there were some to climb!"

"I guess you're hot enough to fuck...

then!" he decided, crawling up over her to wedge his slim, muscular hips into the forked angle of her thighs.

Eagerly, she reached down between them, taking his huge, throbbing cock into her little hand to pull the heavy foreskin back, smoothly, and guiding the blood-filled cock's head directly between her palpitating cunt-lips below.

Not waiting, not caring, he went into her with a headlong rush, just as soon as he felt the tip of his cock touch the velvet-soft flesh of her cuntal opening. The head of his prick, swollen with trapped blood, entered the open, moistly ready channel of her pussy, expanding and pressing aside the vaginal walls with a smooth, sliding action, the thick shaft being absorbed, in its entirety, in her cuntal sheath, as he thrust deeply up into her with a goring, animal-like lunge.

"Ahhhhhhh... My darling!" she moaned as the massive length and breadth of his mighty prick was buried in the resilient softness of her femaleness... to the very core of her vibrant being.

Hunter's body stiffened. "Cut out the darling shit... right now!" he barked. "This's just plain fucking... for the hell of it... understand!?"

She had known what his response would be, but in the rapture of the moment, she had forgotten, the fervent endearment just slipping out, unbidden. "Yes... I understand... H-Hunter!" she murmured, contritely.

The gang leader relaxed... and she knew it would be all right, as she felt the pulsing, rhythmic expansion and contraction of the shaft of his cock against the tightly sheathing walls of her cunt.

The moist heat of her captured and enveloped him, the exquisite folds of her vaginal sheath clamping around the hardness of his prick, the inner muscles of her pussy, caressing and milking at it, tantalizingly, at the same time as he throbbed it, expandingly, deep inside her belly. The sensations were an ecstatic torture to him as he held himself motionless, above her... and his whole being was there, inside her, in the dynamically vibrant power of his cock.

Then, he began to fuck into Billie's clasping cunt with short, quick thrusts, upward into her soft belly, as he held himself aloft on lean, muscular arms, his hips cradled snugly between her legs to ram his ponderous cock home, deep into her softly pulsing vagina.

"Give me all of it!" she gasped. "Deeper! Longer... and faster! I've got to have more cock... in me!"

"All right, Mama... you asked for it!" Hunter grunted, as his huge, blood-inflated prick began to gore deeper and longer into her, its massive girth pulling the soft flanges of her cuntal furrow out with it on each outstroke to reveal the moist, pink lining of her pussy; then, on each plunging instroke, all of it was rammed back up inside of her, again.

Billie could feel all of his length and breadth as his giant cock rampaged in her searingly inflamed cuntal passage, every plundering stroke generating more desire. She couldn't get enough of him, and incessantly she urged him on with groans of pleasure, chanting in tempo with the undulant motion of their bodies, her pelvis moving, now, in wild, abandoned opposition to him, as she fucked back with feral sensuality. "Fuck me! Fuck me... fuckmefuckme! Fuck me... *hard!*" she chanted. It was a hedonistic litany of fuck!

Then, she began to moan with abandon, in ceaseless agony of her impending orgasm. She was there, hanging on the brink of eruptive rapture, as his big cock pounded into her, but she couldn't cum... yet. Finally, she realized that she needed to be in a different position. She had to have the hardness of his plundering prick going into her deeper and harder, with punishing force.

Straining up against him, she splayed her thighs wide and pulled her knees up to her chest. Instantly, Hunter knew what she wanted and stopping only momentarily, he shifted his arms to behind her knees; then, he came back down on her to press her knees back hard to her chest, mashing the tender, swelling mounds of her breasts flat.

Now she was pinned to the sleeping bag like a bug specimen, her loins raised and vulnerable, the whole of her genitals completely available to him for his deepest plundering thrusts. With renewed energy, he rammed his great cock all the way home in her cunt, and his sperm-laden balls smacked, heavily, into the exposed crevice between the fullnesses of her soft, round buttocks.

Billie moved in opposition to him, accepting and absorbing all of his hardened length into her cuntal passage and revelling in the ecstatic pleasure-pain it brought her, as his cock nudged past her cervix, with each bottoming stroke to crash into the farthest back wall of her vaginal vault.

"That's it! That's the way... I want it! All the way!" she urged, glad that she could take all of his cock into her needfully seething cunt. She mewled, gurgled, moaned and groaned with the intensity of her passion, the sounds emitting from deep in her throat, interspersed with sharp gasps of pleasure or pain, as he pistoned, smoothly, in and out of her, almost like a well-oiled machine.

Hunter knew she was going to pop any time, now; as she neared her climax, she continued to mouth obscenities, spurring him on to ever greater effort, her body writhing, uncontrollably, under him, and his own passion rose, spiralingly, toward the summit, where it would end in a final thrusting, jabbing, spewing ejaculation. He was aware that his cock had become even harder and stiffer, expanding to full, lust-engorged erection. The painful need to cum was there, searing him, at the root of his prick. Damn! I've got to pop... pretty soon!

Beneath him, Billie was wild, delirious, her passion completely uncontrolled, as with upturned buttocks, she lay there and took his thundering cock deep into her lust-quivering belly. Nearer and nearer she came to that exquisite moment when delicious, ecstatic orgasm would consume her.

"Oh, Hunter! Fuck hard! Fill my cunt with cock! Fuck it! *Fuck it... fuckitfuckitfuckitfuckitfuckit...* Oh, *fuck!*" she chanted in wild abandon, forcing him to increase his speed, demanding and wanting her release... and she began the giddy spiral, up and up, until suddenly, she stepped out into empty space like an astronaut. Then she was spinning free in timeless space for eons of time... or was it only fractions of seconds?

And, as her release surged through her with electric arcings, her body convulsing with the ecstatic rapture of her orgasm, her throat opened up in a scream of primeval triumph.

"Ahhhhhhhhhhhhhh!"

Even as Billie screamed with the pleasure of her climax, Hunter was goaded on to his own. He was in her, moving faster and faster, longer, harder and deeper, frantically, and his cock, hard as Toledo steel, pistoned the cylinder of her cunt like a run-away steam engine... until finally, he felt the hot, viscous semen jet searingly through the length of his cock, to spew from the slitted tip deep up into the moist warmth of her cuntal sheath. Spasms of pure pleasure coursed through him in mind-boggling, body-satisfying waves of sensuality. Then as his prick continued to pump the last thick drops of his load of sperm from him, he collapsed on top of her with a huge, satiated groan.

"Kerr-rist! That was out of sight... shit, Mama! I'm still cumming!"

Billie could only mewl an unintelligible pleasure-sound, as she struggled with her breathing.

After a few minutes, Hunter rolled himself from on top of her. He was satiated, tired... and sleepy. Billie snuggled in close to him and listened to the sound of his breathing that came deeper and more regular as he drifted off to sleep.

A few moments later, Dipstick MacKay was there, kneeling down beside her and whispering in her ear, "Come on... Billie, baby... get your ass out of there, now! You and me have got some unfinished business!"

"Not right now... Dipstick..." she whispered back. "I'm all tired out..."

"I said... now!" MacKay grated, twisting his hand in her hair and lifting her head up.

Her scalp hurt, and she could do nothing but rise with him, until she was on her knees and finally she was standing before him, naked and helpless.

"You're h-hurting me..." she complained.

"That's nothing to what you'll get... if you don't split with me... right now!"

"Okay... I'll go!" she agreed. "Let me go!"

Dipstick MacKay released her hair, took her by the arm and led her a few paces into the darkness.

Then, he released her arm, sat down on a sleeping bag and began to undress. On the instant he had released her, other hands were on her body, pulling her down to the slick material of the sleeping bag.

"Gavin? Gavin Rust?" she questioned.

"Yeah, baby... none other!"

"A-And Superboy?"

"Who else?" the other voice spat out at her.

They pulled her down to them. Both men were naked, and she was between them, their warm bodies pressed up tight to hers... and she could feel the warm, hard bulk of their cocks against either thigh.

"You're the guest of honour at our little party!" Dipstick MacKay chortled, crawling on top of her.

CHAPTER TWO

Dave and Lauren were quite late arriving at the State Park.

After spending an hour or more in locating a service station that had a proper set of spark plugs for the truck-camper, followed by yet more wasted time, waiting for the attendant to install them, in between pumping gas and servicing other cars, the afternoon had simply slipped away.

Dave had become irritable and grumpy because of the delays, and as they had continued on to the park, he was more snappish with her. He ate the meal she had prepared for him in silence; then he decided that the radio had not been working right. As Lauren tidied up the camper, washing the dishes and cooking utensils, he had taken the radio out of the truck's dash to fix it.

Now, he was fully absorbed in it, tracing out the circuits and testing various parts. Lauren knew that it was one way he had of excluding her. He would be too busy... again...

She hadn't really figured out, yet, what had gone wrong with their marriage. Dave was only thirty years old. He was strong... virile and potent. Sure! He worked hard at a responsible job as shop foreman. But, lately, he had been full of excuses... Lauren was pretty sure that there wasn't another woman although the idea had crossed her mind. God, she'd thought to herself, it'd just kill me... if I ever found out that Dave was s-sleeping with another woman... making l-love to her...

Then, she'd tried to look at herself, objectively. She was only twenty-two, and she knew she was attractive. Always she did everything she could to enhance her loveliness... so she couldn't be driving him away from her on that score.

They argued. Most of their disputes centered around money... and sex. Wryly, she thought about it; the parody was almost comedic. Five years ago, when they were first married, there was too little money... and too much sex... as far as she was concerned. Now, with Dave's promotion to foreman, the financial problems were no longer acute... but sex? Well, it seemed almost as though Dave had lost interest, gradually... until they reached their present state.

That's why she was wearing her tight hot pants. She had bought a couple of pairs, especially for this vacation trip, hoping that showing off her figure to Dave would regenerate some of his former interest. Nothing had happened... yet... at least not with Dave. He had only made some snide remark about not showing her ass like that in public... and to put on something decent.

Yesterday, she remembered she had gotten attention because of her hot pants... but from the wrong man. Ugh! That motorcycle rider... the same one that passed us on the road... and said those awful things to Dave... and made that nasty sign with his hand... He's the same one that was looking at me... and almost undressing me with his eyes! I could almost tell... what he was thinking! She flushed slightly and gave her husband a nervous glance. But he was totally absorbed in his tinkering with the radio, not paying any attention to her at all.

Finishing up her housekeeping chores, Lauren decided she needed some fresh air and an invigorating walk. She put on a light sweater, picked up her purse and told her husband, "I'm going out for a walk, honey. Would you like to go with me?"

"Huh..." Dave looked up at her, reluctantly, "Nahh... you go ahead. I want to finish up on this."

She left the camper, knowing that it would be useless to try getting him interested in her again, tonight. The last time had been the middle of last week! Damn it! She was instantly sorry she had thought it... but that was really what she felt. If I were some kind of an old hag... I could understand it! I want to be a loving... giving wife... but just because I won't let Dave do some of those awful, far-out things to me he gets all upset

– and then he won't do anything! At least, that's what it seems like nowadays.

Deep in thought, she walked along the blacktopped Park Road. No one stirred in the semi-darkness. Tents, campers and trailers were curtained or in had their lights out, and she began to wonder whether or not she might have made a mistake in venturing out.

Suddenly, she stopped dead. A man's voice roared out of the darkness, somewhere over to her right. *"Billie! Get your fucking ass over her... right now!"*

From the slope above, the frightened voice of a girl called back, *"I'm coming! I-I'll be right there, Hunter!"*

The words were shocking. She had no intention of listening to such vulgar people, so she took a few more hesitant steps in the direction she was headed, torn by indecision. Perhaps, she should go back to the camper... but I've only been out here a few minutes. As she walked on, the voices were too low for her to hear, but then the commanding voice of the man came clearly to her again, *"All right... Get those goddamned rags off! I want you bare-ass naked!"*

Now, she knew she didn't want to listen. It must be a man and his wife, she decided... And, he wants to... make love to her! Something like that was too intimate... too personal. I'd die... if I knew somebody were watching or listening to Dave and me!

Lauren stopped, turned around and headed back toward their own campsite. The unseen man's voice cracked out, "NOW... give me your belt!"

The girl's voice trembled, *"P-please Hunter... I-I really didn't hear... Y-you..."*

"I said give me your goddamned belt... Or do you want me to use mine?"

Stopping dead in her tracks, Lauren realized that something was going to happen. It sounded like the man was threatening the girl with a beating. Confirmation of her impression came in the next moment.

"Oh, no! God no!" There was fear in the girl's voice.

"Down on your belly, bitch and take your medicine! And not one squeal... Dig?"

An involuntary gasp escaped Lauren' lips. Oh, God! He is going to beat her... with a belt!

Horrified, she listened, against her will, as the girl pleaded, *"P-please... Don't... Mark me..."*

"You disobeyed me! That's why you're getting it!"

Then, clearly, in the still, night air, Lauren heard the unmistakable crack of leather on bare flesh. She found herself recoiling with each of the three blows. My God!! *What can I do?*

She thought of running back to tell Dave...

try to get him to report it... but there was only a moan from the girl. It must have hurt her... terribly! She didn't leave; instead, she crept closer, her curiosity getting the better of her, and she wondered: What kind of a man... would beat a woman l-like that... and what about the woman who would take it... without crying?

The man rasped, *"That's enough!"* There was silence for a few moments, during which Lauren tried desperately to tear herself away and go back to the camper, but now, she had crept close enough to see the outlines of motorcycles. *Oh! No wonder...* It's those awful people... from that motorcycle gang! There was a terrible feeling of slashing, unreasonable fear that gripped her belly. Dear God! What if he hears me... e-eavesdropping on them? She didn't want to be involved, but the fear of being heard... the possibility of getting caught held her immobile.

"Well... Mama... That ought to be a lesson to you!" The man's voice had an unpleasant tone of self-satisfaction in it.

Lauren knew that she couldn't sneak away without being heard... at least while the couple were silent, so she waited in self-conscious discomfort for them to start talking, again. Her eyes strained in the darkness, until she was barely able to make out the forms of the man and woman. They were on the ground, lying on a sleeping bag. Then, she saw another figure, bulky in leather jacket, sitting on the table, feet on the attached bench, and whoever it was... was watching the couple on the ground... too! From the bulk, the manner of lounging at ease, Lauren decided it must be a man. If she moved, now, made any noise... that unknown watcher would see her, from his vantage point on top of the table. God! Now, she was trapped. She couldn't leave... without being seen or heard!

The man's voice came to her, softer this time.

"You're really hot for my cock, tonight... Eh, mama?"

"Oh, god... Yes! I can't wait for you to... Shove it in... And start fucking me!"

Lauren listened, unwillingly, to the girl, as she mouthed the obscenity, biting back a gasp that came, involuntarily, to her lips. They're going t-to make love... now! But... why would she want to do it... with him... after he beat her... like that? She couldn't fathom it. Understanding of it was beyond her. She didn't want to stay there and listen... B-But... if I leave now... I might get caught... and... She didn't want that. She was sure of it!

After a few moments silence, she heard the unseen, unknown girl say, *"Oh, God... Hunter... I'm so ready for you! Let's fuck...*

Right now!" So... his name is Hunter? I wonder if he's the leader... the one with the big, black beard? She felt the hot flush crawl up her neck to her cheeks, as she remembered: The same one that was practically raping me with his eyes!

"*Well... i'm in the mood for a little cunt-lapping first! you'll really pop, then!*"

The girl spoke, again, after a moment. Her voice was excited... sexy. "*Oh, Hunter... Hunter... I don't care... Whether you fuck it... Or suck it... But p-please... Do something!*"

Lauren saw them move, and she shrank into the shadow of a bush, beside the road, unconsciously, creeping closer, even as her sensibilities were assaulted by the language she had to listen to, as she stood there in the darkness.

"*Oh! Ooooh... God! Hunter! Don't do this... to me! Don't make me wait!*" It was the frantic voice of the girl.

Actually, she couldn't see what they were doing, very clearly, but the girl's next words drew a graphic picture for Lauren. There was no mistaking what they were doing!

"*Ooooooohhh! Yeeeeeessssss! Oh, that's it! Suck me! Lick my pussy... Good! Oh, it feels... So goooooddd!*" The girl's voice was vibrant... exultant with passion. Oh, God... he's really doing it to her... u-using his mouth... on her... h-her g-genitals!

Against her will, Lauren imagined herself there... on the sleeping bag, her thighs spread, obscenely, while that man's tongue licked at her most private parts... and she was suddenly aware of an all-pervading warmth in her loins... and a moistness between her legs that she knew and recognized as sexual arousal. She couldn't believe that it was happening to her. How could... listening to this vulgar filth... m-make me feel this way? *Ugh!* it's so nasty... and vile! How could she like it... so much?

Then, in the stillness of the dark night, Lauren heard obscene sucking sounds. She was sickened... at the same time as the smouldering fire in her own pussy began to burst into an open, naked flame.

"Oooooohhh... My god!" the girl's voice trembled.

Lauren trembled with her, as intense, erotic sensations scorched her belly. Oh, no! It can't be! I can't let myself get all worked up... over something like this! She had to leave, now... before it was too late!

The man sitting on the concrete table top shifted his position, and his head turned in her direction. Oh, God... don't let him see me... here! She tried to make herself invisible, shrinking further into the shadows. The head swiveled back to watch, again, and she heaved a sigh of relief.

Now, the girl, on her back, on the sleeping

bag was pleading with the man she called Hunter, *"Hunter! Oh, Hunter... Use your big cock... Now! Fuck me... In my cunt with your hard cock! Please oh, please! I've got to have your cock... Inside me... Fucking me! Tear me apart with it! Oooooohhhhhhh!"*

"Okay! You're really turned on... Aren't you?"

"Oh, god... I could climb the walls... If there were some to climb!" the girl declared.

"I guess you're hot enough to fuck, then!"

Again, straining her eyes in the darkness, Lauren, who had been an unwilling witness, before, became absorbed in the couple's sexual congress. Never would she have admitted – even to herself – that she was engaging in voyeurism... but she had to see, now! She saw the dim outline of the man's buttocks, as they were raised, then lowered, swiftly, to drive his hardened cock into the girl's vagina. She had to bite back a gasp of her own, as she heard the girl's moan of pleasure, *"Ooooooohhh... Darling!"*

The man's next words shocked her. She had always associated – or equated – love with sex. The girl's 'darling' had seemed so natural. Lauren knew that she would have said the same thing, but Hunter evidently thought otherwise, as he barked, *"Cut out the 'Darling' crap... Right now! This's just plain fucking... For the hell of it... Understand!?"*

Lauren didn't understand... but the unknown girl there on the sleeping bag did, for she murmured, *"yes... I understand... H-Hunter!"* Heavens! Does he mean... he d-doesn't love her... that it's just... nothing but a physical act... just *sex?* When she thought about it, she realized that he had not used any words of endearment. The nearest was his use of Mama, when he addressed her. He hadn't even called her by her name! *No!* That wasn't right; he had called aloud to her, at the very beginning. He had called her Billie. She must be very young!

She saw the rhythmic rise and fall of his buttocks, as he ground into the young girl, Billie, and it was almost as though she were the girl, feeling the throbbing massiveness of the man's penis thrusting in and out of her. God! My imagination's running away... with me! With an effort of will, she told herself that it was just imagination... but at the same time, she knew it was because her own sex-life with Dave was so fraught with uncertainties... and frustrations... and nothings! She had to admit: it was a vicarious sexual pleasure that she was experiencing.

Then, the girl called Billie gasped, *"Give me all of it! Deeper! Longer... and faster! I've got to have more cock... in me!"*

"All right, little Mama... you asked for it!"

The sound of slapping flesh on flesh came clearly to her, as the man and the girl strove together, and as Lauren stood there in the shadows listening and watching, she had an unreasonable wish to be that girl on the sleeping bag. No sooner had the idea formed in her mind than she rejected it. No! Oh, God... NO! What am I thinking? That's monstrous! I couldn't ever do that!

Billie, the girl, urged her lover on to ever-greater effort. *"Fuck me! Fuck me... Fuck me fuck me! Fuck me... Hard!"* It sounded like a chant to Lauren and even though she hated the sound of it, she caught herself repeating it, silently, to herself. Her face flamed with shame. Oh, what's happening to me? I've never even allowed myself t-to think that vile word... before!

Exultant, now, Billie told him, *"That's it! That's the way... I want it! All the way!"*

Unbidden, uncontrolled, Lauren's own hand sought for and found the heated triangle between her thighs, as unconsciously she caressed and massaged herself. Again, she caught herself and was horrified to discover what she was doing. It was a self-revelation. She had never done it, before, and she snatched her hand away. That's horrible... and so wrong! But, I-I can't help it! I'm so hot... so worked up over this! If I could only leave... now... without being seen...

Again, Billie began to chant her need.

"Oh, Hunter! Fuck hard! Fill my cunt... With cock! Fuck it! Fuck it! Fuckitfuckitfuck itfuckitfuckit... Oh, fuck!"

Silently, her mind reeling, Lauren repeated it: Fuck it! Fuck it! Oh, God... *I* want it! *I* want to be fucked *too!*

Then, the girl on the sleeping bag was screaming out her orgasm. *"Aaaaaaaauuuuo oooogggghh!"*

Standing there in the darkness, it was almost too much for Lauren. Her hand was, once again, massaging frantically at her own pussy, as she watched the rise and fall of Hunter's buttocks pounding his cock into the convulsing girl like a jackhammer, until suddenly, he collapsed on top of her and lay still. His voice rasped out, *"Kerr-ist! That was out of sight... shit, Mama! I'm still cumming!"*

Lauren stood there, almost hypnotically rubbing herself, feeling the arcing sensations in her belly... the burning fires of sexual arousal that cold be extinguished in only one way... by a hard, thrusting cock! For one mind-boggling instant, she entertained the insane idea that she wanted to strip off her clothing, fling herself down on that sleeping bag, spread her thighs in obscene invitation... and take that girl's place under the man called Hunter. She smothered a gasp of horror that she could even have thought such a monstrous thing. Oh, God...

No! That's crazy! It could never happen to me, because I'd never *let* it happen!

Now the man seated on the campsite tabletop climbed down and began to walk toward the couple on the sleeping bag. This was her chance to escape... and she took it. Walking softly, she gained the road, being careful not to scuff her feet or stumble... until she was well away; then she ran back to their camper, glad that she had been able to get away without being discovered.

She sat down at the table provided for their campsite, knowing that she would have to calm herself... before she went inside the camper.

She couldn't tell Dave about what she had seen... and especially, she couldn't explain to him – or to anyone, for that matter – the effect her watching and listening had had upon her.

But maybe – if she were lucky – she could somehow get Dave aroused to the point where he would want to put out the fire in her belly.

She knew exactly what she wanted – and needed. It was the hardness of her husband's stiff penis deep in her vagina that she desired so much. Her mind was in a turmoil; her stomach churned, while below, between her legs, delicious sensations still coursed, unchecked, reminding her of her great need. *Oh, what can I do to get him to fuck me?* She had heard that word so often, in the last few minutes that she had thought it, again, and her face flamed to think she had used it so easily. Her husband, Dave, used the word, of course, and she always cringed, inwardly, when he did. Now her own mind was cluttered up with the vile vulgarity. *What's happening to me?*

In a few minutes, Lauren had got her breath under control, smoothed down her run-away emotions and rationalized away her temporary, vicarious involvement with the couple on the sleeping bag. She shamed herself for being a curious voyeur, promising herself that it would never happen, again.

Then, she went to the door of their camper, opened it and went inside, a radiant smile on her face. Going to Dave, she impulsively threw her arms around him, from the back and kissed him on the neck. "It's just lovely out tonight!" she said, lightheartedly. "You should have gone with me!" Maybe, came the unbidden thought, he would've gotten hot if he had heard and seen what she had!

Dave was annoyed by her interruption. "Yeah I suppose... but watch it... I've just about got this damned radio fixed... and I don't want to lose any parts!" He shrugged her away.

Reluctantly, her heart almost breaking at his rebuff, she sat down opposite him and tried to show interest in what he was doing.

Finally, he announced that it was repaired. "I'll put it back in place in the morning." He got up, stretched and yawned. "I think I'll go down to the bath house and take a shower..."

"Okay, darling..." Lauren agreed, "and while you're gone... I'll get ready for bed. I brought that new, shorty nightgown along... would you like for me to... wear it tonight?" She made her voice suggestive.

"Hell, I don't care! Wear what you want to!" he grunted, disinterestedly, heading for the door with his towel in hand.

She hid her disappointment and added, "I-I thought maybe you and I could, you know, have some fun... tonight."

"I've had a pretty hard day. Sorry, but I'm kind of tired..." And with that, he left the camper.

Tears glistened in her eyes. There was still an aching need in her loins, and warm sensations of sexual arousal still smouldered there, doused down slightly, but ready, on the instant, to burst back into a consuming, raging fire of passion.

Having showered earlier in the evening, it didn't take her long to undress; putting on a little perfume and the frilly, see-through nightgown, she turned off most of the lights and crawled up into the big bunk that jutted out over the cab of the truck. She was determined that she would make herself provocative, desirable. Somehow, she had to make Dave realize her need, make him want to make love to her tonight. *I just don't understand what's happened to him to us! Oh, it would be so wonderful to be able to make love as free and easy as those people were tonight!*

Then, she remembered:... *But, heavens... I'd almost forgotten! He beat her with a belt; then he used his mouth on her genitals, licking and sucking her down there! Ugh! I don't see how that could be very nice... but that girl, Billie, seemed to like it so much! Maybe if I...* But Lauren Christie couldn't get beyond the 'maybe'. There was just no way, she decided, that she would ever allow that!

Soon, she was going over more of the details of what she had heard and seen, the memories working deep in her, and before she realized it, libidinous sensations were coursing through her, again... and she could hardly wait for Dave to return from his shower.

When she heard him at the door, she leaned up on one elbow, arranging herself, fetchingly, hoping he wouldn't ignore her and praying that he would change his mind.

Dave chose to ignore her. She watched as he changed into his pajamas and was dismayed, when he began to make up the smaller bunk, converted from the breakfast nook area.

"Wh-why are you going to sleep down there... by yourself?" Lauren asked her husband, dismally.

"I told you, God damn it! I'm tired... and we've got a lot of miles to cover, tomorrow!" He turned out the light and crawled into the single bunk.

Lauren pulled up the light blanket, feeling completely rejected – again! Tears streamed from her eyes... but she would not cry aloud. She wouldn't let him know how much he had hurt her. All she had wanted from him was his husbandly love.

And, she had love to spare, to give him, in return. She had this beautiful body, clean, healthy, vibrant and aching to be loved. Unconsciously, her hands drifted up under the flimsy material of her nightgown to cup the soft fullnesses of her breasts, the magnificent orbs springy and pliant in her palms. The hardened cones of her nipples were sensitive in her fingers, as she rolled them, caressingly. "Oh, God... I'm so aroused... so hot for Dave... but there's nothing I can do to get him... to f-fuck me!"

She winced at her involuntary use of 'that' word. As her hands wandered, then, down over the gentle curvature of her belly, to the golden triangle of her loins, and she felt the searing sensations of need that flared there, out of control, she slipped a finger down into the furrow, parting the soft fuzz of hair to find the firm little shaft of her clitoris. Her touch there caused her to gasp with ecstasy.

She had never done it to herself... but as she massaged, delicately, along the short length of the erectile bud, she knew, suddenly, that it was one way, at least, of gaining the release from the sexual tension built up in her. It was wrong! She knew it... but... I've got to do something... or I'll go out of my mind!

On the bunk, below, she heard Dave's soft snore. He was sound asleep. She knew then that she would do it. She did!

Lauren was so aroused that with only a little more manipulation of her clitoris, she came to climax, convulsively, and she had to stuff the corner of a pillow into her mouth to keep from screaming aloud.

Then, as she relaxed in the wash of the euphoria of sexual satiety, she marveled, at what had happened to her. She was almost proud with what she had done for herself, but it was short-lived as her conscience soon regained the moral high ground, again, punishing her, scourging her... for what she believed to be a trespass.

Her sleep was fitful and restless, and she dreamed a bizarre dream. She was naked, tied hand and foot, her legs spread wide, while a fiend, a veritable monster, tantalized her, sexually. The man-monster had a huge black beard.

Leeringly, he told her exactly what he was going to do to her... and in the dream, Lauren wanted him to do it; she wanted him to do every vile thing to her... that he could think of doing.

Just as the fiend with the black beard lowered his mouth to her seething vagina to lick and suck her there, he was changed, in a twinkling... and it was her husband, Dave, who knelt between her legs, his face only inches above her loins.

"No!" she screamed. "You can't do that... t-to me!"

Lauren woke up!

Oh, God! It was only a dream...

But, it seemed so real! Suddenly, she was aware that her hand was clamped tightly between her legs. She decided that was the cause of the dream... and she felt some relief.

Then, she wondered:... But, in the dream... it seemed to be all right... for that horrible man to do it to me... and I wouldn't let Dave do it! *Why not?* Oh God! I'm really so mixed up!

Highway to Shame 57

CHAPTER THREE

In the big double bunk of their trailer Artie Berman finished off the last gulp of his Scotch, set the glass aside, wiped his mouth on the back of his hand and reached out for his wife, Zoe.

"Come here, damn it! I'm in the mood for a piece of ass!" he told her.

Zoe was bitchy, tonight. "What's the matter, honey... you losing your touch?"

She was sitting on the edge of the bed pulling off her slacks, when her husband wrapped his brawny arms around her and pulled her back toward him, to plaster his lips to hers. After a moment or two, she squirmed away from him.

"Now... what in hell does that remark mean?" Artie growled, scratching his hairy chest. He lay nude in the bunk, big and bulky, his green eyes flashing a mean anger.

"Well..." she chided, half-kidding him, now, as she saw that he had taken her remark too seriously. "We've been on our vacation for three days... and nothing's happened... yet!"

"It's a little different!" he explained. "But I spotted a doll, today... and she's right here in this camp ground!"

"Well?"

"I thought I'd go to work on it... tomorrow!"

Zoe had been undressing while they were talking, and Artie watched her, avidly; he never failed to get a real charge out of watching his wife undress. She was down to her panties and bra, now. From long practice, he reached out to unclasp the hooks at the back, slid the garment over her arms and captured a bountiful, white breast in each big paw of a hand.

"Are you going to keep it a big secret... about who she is?"

"Hell... I don't know her name, yet!" Artie kneaded his wife's breasts, feeling their satiny smoothness, the berry-like nipples just beginning to become hard and erect.

"Since when does that bother you, Artie?" she asked, wriggling dexterously from his grasp and standing up to peel her panties down over the swelling curves of her hips and buttocks. She always managed to make this simple movement a sexy ritual, and Artie watched her with concentrated attention, his penis jerking with mounting excitement, as the black, silky hair of her pubic mound was exposed to his lewd gaze.

"It doesn't... really!"

"Yes... I know... only too well! Is she blonde, brunette... or what?"

"She's a true blonde, I think. She's the one I remarked about... when I saw her at that service station... remember? In that little town... about sixty miles back!"

"The one in the camper they were fixing there?"

"The same. She was wearing those tight hot pants!"

"Oh, yes... I remember! And I'll have to do something about that!" she smiled.

"What do you mean?"

"I'm going to buy some hot pants... the first chance I get!"

"There you go... wanting to spend some more money... for something you don't need!"

Zoe smiled, coyly, and countered with, "Well... I've got to compete... somehow!"

"You don't need them! I like you better... without pants!" His eyes roamed over his wife's luscious body. "Now... come here, damn it... or I'm coming after you!"

She regarded him, coolly, through narrowed gray eyes and tossed back a stray strand of jet black hair, as her eyes zeroed in on the rampant, hardened length of his cock that stood out, yearningly, from his hairy loins. "Why, Artie... my darling husband... I do believe you've got something there for me tonight!"

Crawling onto the bed, she came up over him to capture his spearing prick between her legs, then clamping her thighs together tight around it she lay full length on top of him, the full orbs of her magnificent breasts mashing down against his big, hairy chest.

She lowered her head, her mouth finding his to weld them together in a deep, soul kiss. Her tongue ventured far into his mouth to be sucked and nibbled. Below, she felt the throbbing length of his big cock, where it lay, log-like, tight up against the sensitive flesh of her slit.

Artie enveloped her in his muscular arms, squeezing her to him hard, then, his hands began to roam down over the smoothness of her back to the full, mounding protuberances of her buttocks. His fingers dug into the satiny, resilient flesh to knead and massage, caressingly. Damn! She was still the most sexually exciting woman he had ever known and he had known quite a few... But, hell they're just the frosting on the cake! Zoe's the meat and potatoes... and she's right here... ready to fuck... anytime I want her!

He savored the sweetness of her mouth, sucking and nibbling on her tongue then, after a few moments, used his own to burst into her mouth. His big cock was jerking and throbbing between her legs, and he could feel the building warmth in her pussy.

Abruptly, Zoe raised her head and broke the moist, open-mouthed kiss. "Did you notice him? What's he like?" she asked.

"Who in the hell are you talking about?"

"The blonde's husband, stupid!"

"Oh, him?" Artie grunted. "He's just an ordinary guy medium height and build...

around thirty maybe a little more, wears eyeglasses…"

"That's what I was afraid of!" she pouted.

"What's that?" He tried to pull her mouth down to his; at the same time he began to saw his big cock back and forth in her moistly throbbing furrow.

She resisted him long enough to answer, "You always pick out these fabulous women for yourself… and they always seem to turn out having just ordinary husbands! It's not fair!"

"Well, hell… I guess that's just the breaks!" He pulled her down, hard, and kissed her with open mouth and probing tongue.

Zoe mumbled around his tongue, "Someday… Artie, darling… I'm going to reverse that on you."

"The hell you say!"

His hard hands smoothed down over her full-rounded buttocks that were now gyrating against the shaft of his massively solid cock that lay the length of her pulsing cuntal furrow. Their mouths were welded together, tongues searching and savouring, and his hands dug in with strong-fingered kneading of the pliant flesh of the twin orbs that moved so lithely against him.

After a few moments, Artie decided it was time for his little surprise. Deftly, he rolled his wife to her back, reached under his pillow and grasped the object he had hidden there earlier in the evening. Zoe kept her eyes closed as he continued to kiss her, then surreptitiously, he brought his hand down until it was just above her pubic mound, the bullet shaped, battery-powered vibrator aimed right at her slightly exposed slit. Just as it touched her, he flipped the switch on and ran the ogive-shaped, vibrating head down between her legs to contact her already hardened clitoris.

Zoe's eyes flew open with surprise. She knew what it was instantly, as the vibrator sent exquisite sensations flashing through her whole body. She shivered with delight, and a moan came from her lips, as she broke the wet contact of their kiss.

"Oh, Artie... you did bring it!" she exulted.

"No... this one's new! It's got batteries in it!"

"Oh, it feels wonderful... darling!"

Zoe's clear gray eyes smouldered up at him, as below, her white, tapering thighs parted to allow him full access to her throbbing pussy, her hips already undulating with building sexual arousal.

"I thought maybe you'd like it!" Artie rumbled, directing the smooth, plastic vibrator down through the ultra-sensitive furrow of her cunt until the bullet-like head was lined up with her vaginal opening. He heard her mewl with pleasure, and her loins rose to meet it. Holding the vibrating dildo in place, steadily, he looked down to watch her gyrating hips as she tried to capture it.

"Don't tease me... Harrrry! Shove it in! I want to feel it up inside of me!"

"Okay... on one condition!" he bargained.

"What's that?"

"Suck me off!"

"Oh, yessss... darling! You know I'll do it for you... any time!" she agreed.

"I just wanted to make sure you would!"

Then, with a swift jabbing motion, he shoved the dildo deeply into his wife's cuntal passage, as far as it would go. He knew she'd like it that way. She had really learned to turn on... fast, since getting that first vibrator. Hell! It's just a matter of training... or conditioning! He held it deep in her passage, for a moment or two, watching as her cunt lips moved back, as she screwed her hips back and down into the mattress, then nibbled their way back up the vibrating shaft, erotically.

The dildo, vibrating deep in her belly, produced almost instantaneous ecstasy for Zoe. The powerful sensations swept through her like a tidal wave, and she responded to it with a deliciously soaring joy. Her head began to thrash back and forth on the pillow, her jet-black hair becoming entangled, strands of it sweeping across her distorted face.

"Oh, God!" she moaned. "Fuck me with it... now Artie! I'm going... to cum... very, very soon!"

He began to thrust the vibrating surrogate cock in and out of her voracious, heated cunt, simulated the natural motions of a penis. From experience, he knew it really wouldn't be very long until she exploded in orgasm.

It hadn't always been that way for her. He remembered: Hell! A year ago she didn't like to fuck hardly at all! But, she learned! Christ when I used the vibrator on her that first time... and she found out she could cum... any time she wanted... and just keep on cumming... if she wanted to... there's been no stopping her! Then, there had been the experiments with swapping... And, since we've been doing the swinging thing... joining up with the club... and all... she can't get enough fucking... and that's just the way I like it!

His wife began to gasp, her breath coming in short, jerky pantings. "Faster! Deeper!" she demanded.

Kneeling above her, then, Artie began to thrust it in and out of her demanding cunt with more force, pushing the electric phallus into her as far as he could. With his other hand he reached down to the silky black hair of her pubic mound and used a finger, lightly, on the blood-distended shaft of her clitoris, rubbing across it in tempo with the fucking motion in and out of her cuntal passage. As he knelt there, between his wife's lovely legs, manipulating her to orgasm, his lanced-out, hardened cock jerked and throbbed, involuntarily, with the eroticism of his act. He was hot... ready to fuck, but he could wait, he decided. It'll be like heaven... when she gets her mouth to working on me!

Suddenly, she was there! She came convulsively, her body shuddering with delicious rapture, as her release washed over her body. *"Oh God, Arrrtieeee!* Oh, darling... that's it! I'm *cumming! I'm cumming! Aughhh! Ohhhh!"*

Her legs splayed to either side, and as Artie watched, he saw her face contort in exquisite agony... then begin to relax into beatific beauty, again, as the euphoria of her rapture overcame her. He pulled the vibrating dildo from her clasping cuntal passage, switched it off and tossed it aside on the bed. Coming down on top of her then, he kissed her lips, tenderly, and held her tight while her quivering body gradually relaxed.

After a few moments, she opened her eyes and mumbled against his mouth, "Oh... that one was nice, darling, but later on tonight, I want you to fuck me, too!"

"Okay, doll! Anything you say!" He laughed, rolling from on top of her and sprawling out on his back beside her; then he went on to ask, "That remark you made... about getting even with me... you don't have any ideas about picking up guys, on your own do you?"

"Oh... that! Well, not that I haven't been tempted, but I saw a guy that I could really go ape over!" she explained, her eyes lighting up, as she remembered. "And, there'd be a sweet, young thing for you!"

"How young?"

"Oh, like maybe seventeen or eighteen!"

"And the guy's a young kid I suppose?"

"He looks older... maybe twenty-five..."

"All right," Artie growled, "don't keep me in suspense! Who the hell are they?"

"He's the one on the motorcycle... with the girl riding behind him... remember?"

"Christ, Zoe!" he exploded. "You can't be serious! We don't want to get mixed up with any of them!"

"Why not?"

"Hell! Those people ride in gangs... and pull all kinds of cruddy things! I wouldn't trust them further than I can see them... or smell them! He was the one with the black beard and acted like the leader... right?"

"Yes... that's him!" she affirmed. "But, I think it'd be fun... to get to know somebody like that!"

"It could be dangerous, too!" her husband exploded. "And I say no, we're not going to get involved with them! We'll stick to our own kind!"

Zoe decided to needle him. "And what kind is that, darling?"

"The safe kind!" he growled. "Middle class... white... you know what I mean!"

"Yes, I know what you mean: WASPS – is that it? White, Anglo-Saxon and Protestant!" She was sarcastic. "Your prejudices are showing!"

Artie didn't want to argue with her, just then. He had a big, solid hard-on... and he was more interested in sex than he was in her views about his prejudices. "Hell, Zoe! I don't want to fight with you about some stupid thing... right now! Let's finish what we started... Okay?"

"Okay, honey," she agreed, softening, as she realized she was being unnecessarily sharp about it. She knew her husband's point of view. It just didn't always agree with her own, more liberal, outlook. "Can I ask you one thing, though? What about the blonde... and her husband? How are we going to get to meet them and?"

"Christ I told you... I was going to work on it, tomorrow! When he gets up in the morning his truck's not going to start... then I'm going to be on hand to help him fix it!"

"You mean you've already fixed it so it won't start?"

"Hey... you got it... the first time!" he

complimented her, sarcastically. "I switched some wires around and when he isn't looking... I put them back which makes me a mechanical genius... then we have a drink... and we take it from there!"

"Okay, I understand, Artie." She smiled up at him, sparklingly. "I'll do my part, even if he is kind of... ordinary."

She kneeled up and crawled over between his legs. He spread them out wider for her, and as he looked down the length of his body to watch her, he saw that his cock no longer was standing up rigid and hard. It leaned, crazily, to one side, as it became detumescent.

"Shit! All this damn talking made me lose my hard-on!" he grumbled, complainingly.

"Don't worry, darling!" Zoe told her husband. "I'll fix that right away!" Her eager hand reached down to grip the almost flaccid shaft of his cock. She held it upright and felt the throbbing growth of it her touch had caused; then, deftly, she milked the heavy foreskin back over the rapidly inflating corona. "See... it's coming to life... already!" she exulted.

Artie raised his hips up to her, driving the shaft of his cock into the grip of her hand and felt a certain pride to see it soar out several inches beyond her grasping thumb and forefinger. Meanwhile, her other hand went lower, under him, to caress his heavy, sperm-heavy balls, her fingernails scratching lightly over the taut but crinkled surface of his scrotal sac.

Then, she leaned down, lower, to kiss the satiny, mauvish tip of his cock. God! It felt good. He felt the powerful pulse of furiously pumping blood at the electrifying touch of her lips.

Knowing the stimulating effect of it, Zoe used her teeth to lightly nip up and down the hardening length of his prick. His groan of pleasure urged her on, as she switched sides, nibbling a little harder, now. She spotted the battery-powered vibrator, her husband had tossed aside and wondered what effect it would have on him. She took it in her hand, found the switch and turned the device on, then she brought the humming, oval head of it into contact with his testicles, running it gently over them.

Artie's body jerked. "Christ!" he grunted. "I don't know how much of that I could take!"

"Does it feel good... darling!"

"Too damn good! It feels like it'd make me cum... in about fifteen seconds!"

Experimentally, then, she ran it lower, until it was grazing the brownish, crinkled flesh of his anal opening. The vibrator made him jump, again, as powerful sensations flooded through him, and his massive cock began to throb, violently, in her hand. "Take it away!" he ordered. "It's too much! Too much!"

"Okay!" She snapped it off. "Now... you know what it does to me!"

"Yeah... but you can just keep cumming! A man can't do that! There's a need for a little rest in between times, so it's different!"

Tossing the vibrator to the foot of the big, double bunk bed, she held his pulsing cock in both hands, and her honeyed mouth came down to it, her ovaled lips encompassing the bloated head with warm moistness. Involuntarily, his prick kept jerking in her mouth, and the very thought of what she was doing gave him a large, erotic charge, as usual. It was the lewdness, the salaciousness of it, almost as much as the intensity of the keening sensations her mouth brought him, that seemed to increase his pleasure in it, giving him an added sense of voluptuousness.

Now, she held the massive length of his cock with one hand, again, while the other massaged and gently palpated his balls below, caressingly, being careful not to hurt them; meanwhile, her cheeks began to hollow as she sucked on the head of his cock, rhythmically.

"God! That's sweet! You're mouth's just like honey... Zoe!" he moaned.

Her head began to bob up and down on him, her mouth absorbing more and more of his hard flesh with each steady stroke, while inside, her tongue swirled in wild circles around his throbbing cock's head. On the up-strokes he felt her trying to force the tip of her tongue into the split at the top.

Tensing his loins, he thrust his hips up at her face to drive his prick deeper into her mouth and throat. He saw it all go in... all the way to the root, as her nose was mashed into the curly cushion of his pubic hair. With a moan, he began to move in and out of her mouth, in rhythmic counterpoint to her bobbing head, her mouth a substitute cunt.

Artie was lost in a morass of all-consuming, pleasure sensations, centered there in his cock in Zoe's mouth. He watched almost as though he were in a trance, as her mouth began to move up and down the length of his shaft with increasing speed and pressure, her tongue executing an extra swirling lick to his lust-inflated cock's head on every outward stroke, and her lips seeming to nibble their way back, again, as she took his cock deep into her throat without gagging even once.

His wife's face, working over his loins was changed, and he realized that she, too, was in a sexual rapture of her own. Her eyes were closed. Her nostrils flared delicately as she had to breathe through her nose. It never failed to amaze him. Damn! She puts so much into it... now! He was glad, all over again, that he was still married to her. God! And, we came so close to calling it quits!

Then her long, straight black hair fell softly, in lustrous cascades, into his naked lap. The sensation was provocative, almost maddening, and he reached out to her head with both hands to guide her up and down the demanding shaft of his throbbing cock. Ever more forcefully he thrust his hips up at her, driving his cock, relentlessly, into her mouth, and he watched with fascination as little ragged flanges of the inside of her lips was pulled out to slide along his length on each upward bob of her head, then it was all stuffed back in again, as her head came downward and he thrust up hard at her face. Her cheeks hollowed, too, as she continued to suck hungrily on him.

Suddenly, all the gathering sensations were concentrated in the blood-inflated head of his cock. He felt it jerk and throb, insanely, and it seemed to grow larger with every ecstatic pulse, and all the while his wife's tongue swirled over its frenulum, swooped around its flange and stiffened to titillate the twitchy little slit of its meatus.

He knew he would have to cum... soon. It was getting nearer, for he could feel the searing burn of it deep in his groin, as the impatiently waiting load of sperm began to demand its release, like a broad, deep river pushing with relentless force against the face of a mighty dam.

Words tumbled from his mouth.

"Oh, fuck... that's good! A little more... just a little more... Zoe... and I'll cum! Just a little... while... now! *Aaaaauuuuuuggghh!* Shit!"

Strangling, unintelligible sounds replaced the words. He gasped for breath. It was almost there... for him! He was going to cum... now! Furiously, he rammed his hips up against his wife's sucking mouth, fucking blindly, animalistically, now, into the surrogate cunt of her oral cavern. He looked down to see the steel-hard rigidity of his spewing cock go all the way to the hilt. She had taken all of him... every last fraction of an inch. Her nose was mashed flat against the hardness of his pubic bone, and he saw that she was struggling with her breathing at the same time as she attempted to swallow his copious ejaculate.

"Now!" he grunted in needless warning. "I'm cumming... *now!*"

His sperm pumped through him, explosively; the jet of hot, white viscous semen hosed through the length of him to spray from the slitted tip in the lust-bloated head of his cock deep into the honeyed moistness of her frantically gulping throat.

Roughly, his hard hands on her head pulled her mouth down hard on his spewing prick, and his hips moved, spasmodically, up at her, driving his cock deep into her throat, immobilizing her, as he shot his cum into her

mouth, forcing her to swallow his thick, gluey liquid to keep from gagging. It lasted for several cruel moments, until at last his body relaxed and he flopped back on the bed with a loud groan of satisfaction.

Then, gently now, realizing that he had treated her more roughly than he had intended, his hands traced down across her cheeks, and he moaned, "Zoe... honey... that was out of this world!"

By degrees, his big cock began to deflate in her mouth, but she kept sucking and nibbling on it until every drop of his sperm had been consumed; then, sighing, audibly, she raised her head to look up the barrel-chested, hairy length of his body, as at the same time, she allowed his flaccid, detumescent penis to pull from her mouth. It glistened in the dim light from the moisture of her saliva.

"I'm glad you liked it, darling..." she murmured, looking at him through hot, smouldering eyes. Then, as she slithered up over him, she asked, "Would you like to have a drink... before I hold you to your promise?"

"Okay!" he agreed. "Mine's double Scotch... on the rocks!"

CHAPTER FOUR

While Lauren tidied up inside the camper, after breakfast, getting everything ship-shape for travel, Dave Christie put the repaired radio back into the dash and tried it out. He listened, critically, and decided that his tinkering with it had improved the reception. Satisfied with his work, he then checked the outside of the camper, looking at the tires and making sure all was in readiness for travel.

He went to the door, at the rear of the camper, and called inside to his wife, "Are you ready to go, Lauren?"

"In just a minute..." she called out, forcing a cheerfulness into her voice that she didn't really feel.

"Well... hurry it up! I'm all set to roll!"

Lauren didn't really like the way their vacation was going. They hadn't stopped to enjoy any of the sights. It was just go, go, go! Dave seemed to be more interested in covering miles than enjoying scenery. She had suggested stopping for more than one night, but he had cut her off, curtly, not really listening to her at all. He was going to do it his way... and that's all there was to it!

Finishing up the last of her chores, she came out into the bright morning sunshine. Dave closed and locked the door and settled down into the driver's seat of the truck, while

Lauren clambered up to sit beside him.

Dave turned the ignition key. The starting motor whirred, turning the engine over. It didn't start.

"The damn motor must be colder than I thought!" he growled.

He tried it four more times before he decided there must be something wrong. As he climbed from the cab to open the hood, his temper was short. He peered into the engine compartment, attempting to spot the trouble.

Artie Berman, who had been watching for some minutes now, chose this time to saunter down the road, and as Dave raised the hood, Artie was there, in a moment, to peer inside with him.

"Trouble?" Artie queried.

Dave looked up with annoyance.

"Yeah... the damned thing won't start for some reason!"

"Plenty of gas?"

"Yeah... I filled up, yesterday."

"The battery's okay... I heard it turning over..."

"It's not firing... at all!" Dave grumbled, examining some of the ignition wires.

"Why don't you try it, again... and I'll watch and listen to see if I can spot your trouble..." Artie suggested.

Looking up to see the interested and concerned stranger, Dave saw a big, bluff, barrel-chested man, greying slightly at the temples, who smiled at him through friendly green eyes. The man's hands, resting on the truck's fender, looked hard and capable, and Dave was glad of the help offered.

"Okay!" He got into the driver's seat, again, and turned the ignition key. The engine turned over with the starter, but still did not catch.

Under the hood, out of Dave's sight, Artie switched a wire back to its original place. The motor made encouraging sounds of starting.

"Oh, there you are, Artie... I've been looking all over for you!" It was a beautiful, black-haired woman dressed in tight slacks and halter top who walked up to the camper.

"Hi... Zoe... I'm just helping this gentleman get his truck started."

Lauren got out of the cab and Zoe came around to the door to meet her. "Hello..." she said, pleasantly, "We're the Christies. I'm Lauren... and that's my husband, Dave."

Dave got out of the cab and joined the others. Introductions were made, and the two men went back to the problem of the non-starting engine.

"I just jiggled a couple of wires... a while ago... maybe that's all that's wrong..." Artie observed. "Let's try it, again!"

"I was just trying to convince Artie... that's

it's too nice a day to just travel. I'm trying to get him to stay here in the park for another day, at least..." Zoe said, conversationally, to Lauren, as the two women stood aside to watch.

"That's what I'd like to do, too!" Lauren agreed. "But... Dave wants to keep moving..."

Artie switched another ignition wire. The engine coughed a couple of times and started. "That's it!" Artie called out.

Dave left the engine running and came to the front of the truck, again. Artie's wife was talking to him, urgently, trying to convince him of something, so he stood back waiting for them to finish. He wanted to thank his benefactor and be on his way. While he waited, he couldn't help noting the magnificent figure her clothing did little to hide. Damn! She's quite a woman... and she's got it all in the right places!

Finally, their low-voiced conversation finished, Artie Berman smiled at his wife and said, "Well... if that's really what you want... I guess I could try!"

Coming up to the big man, then, Dave began, "Mr. Berman I certainly do thank you... for..."

"Aw, hell don't thank me for anything! I just fiddled around with the ignition wires a little bit..." he rumbled, dismissing the subject. "Now... my wife, Zoe's been after me to stay here in the park for another day... and she wants me to invite you and your wife to go around and see the sights with us!"

"That's very nice... but..."

"Really... Mr. Christie..." Zoe broke in. "Your wife and I were talking about it... and we both felt the same way... about staying here!"

"It's easy for me to unhitch our car... to drive around in!" Artie added.

"Let's do it, Dave!" Lauren enthused. "It'd be a lot of fun!"

"Besides... I like to make new friends!" Zoe smiled, directing a smoky gaze at Dave, her eyes sweeping over him, appreciatively. *He's not too bad, really! In fact he looks better... the more I see of him!*

Her hot look was not completely wasted on Dave. He understood it. She was interested in him... but what he didn't understand was the open way in which she did it. That bothered him – not that he was interested – but just on the principle of it. He sure as hell wouldn't want Lauren going around giving guys – especially strange guys – that sort of come-on look! Christ!

"We could have dinner... somewhere... together..." Artie invited.

"Maybe a few drinks?" Zoe suggested.

"Well... I don't know..." Dave was undecided. That open invitation in Zoe's provocative look was tempting... but...

"It's vacation time... and we go out so seldom... Dave! Why don't we do it?"

"There're a lot of interesting things we can do." It was Zoe, again. Her tongue flicked out to lick her lips. Dave was sure it was a second signal, not just coincidence. It was too sensually fraught with meaning. *Damn it... I wonder if its for real... or is she just a teaser!?*

"All right!" His mind was made up, then. "We'll stay and see the sights with you, but let me stand the dinner, tonight in appreciation for your help just now, Mr. Berman!"

"Let's knock off that Mister stuff! I'm just plain old Artie to my friends!" Berman grinned jovially. "And I'll call you Dave... Okay? And, your lovely wife?"

"Lauren," Dave answered, noticing that the other man's eyes swept like a lingering caress over her body.

"And I'm Zoe!" Her smile was dazzling.

It didn't take them long to get organized. Cameras and light sweaters were loaded into the Bermans' car, which was quickly and easily unhitched from the trailer, and the two couples were off to do the things tourists do.

They followed the map printed in a park brochure, driving to lookout points and various natural attractions of the area. The conversation sparkled, as it always does when people are newly acquainted, comparing views, relating experiences... getting to know more about each other.

Several times, as they walked to or stood at guard rails enjoying the panorama of the vista point, Zoe's body brushed against Dave's, and once, as he stood behind her, her hand swept across his groin, accidentally; however, the caressing feel she gave him, with her fingers, told him it was on purpose. It bothered him. Christ! I really do wonder now, what is her game? The thing that really made him cautious was that she did it in front of her husband. Oh, she's sneaky about it, but hell, I don't want to get involved, in any way with any woman while her husband's around! What's she thinking about, anyway?

He was flattered, of course, but his built-in sense of decency wouldn't allow him even to think about a dalliance, attractive and beautiful as Zoe Berman was! The first chance I get, I'll have to put her straight! She's wasting her time, as long as Lauren – and Artie Berman – are in the picture!

Artie stopped for lunch in the village, insisting the four of them all have a full meal instead of a snack. He ordered up martinis to sharpen their appetites. As they had gotten into the booth, Zoe sat next to Dave. He was uncomfortable about it, especially when he felt the long, warm taper of her thigh pressed close against his.

Dave tasted his martini. It was good; then, as he tried to follow some conversational gambit of Artie's, a long, involved story concerning some happening in his work, Zoe's hand stole over to his thigh, her fingers feathering upward toward his crotch. Damn! She's persistent! And, there was no doubt in his mind, any longer, concerning her intentions.

Her little innuendos, touchings and nudgings began to pay-off for Zoe now. As she brushed upward, ever so lightly, she detected a responsive twitch, transmitted through the material of his trousers and she knew that she had made some progress. His cock's getting hard now! It's going to be fun to get him up when he can't do anything about it! Then later, when I get him alone... *Mmmmmm!* It'll be real yummy!

Now, her hand lay gently upon his groin, her fingers tracing the outline of his hardening penis inside his pants. She tried to calculate its dimensions as she felt along it's hot length. There's nothing ordinary about this.

Above, widely innocent grey eyes seemingly concentrated on her husband's lengthy story, Dave stole a sidelong glance at her profile. Christ! She's really playing with fire! He decided, then, that her little games would have to come to an end... at least until he could talk to her. There was no way he'd play... unless he knew what the ground rules were. The way she's going at it... almost anything could happen... if her husband found out!

Firmly, he grasped her wrist, under the table... and with equal firmness, resolutely, returned her hand to her own lap. Zoe turned and smiled, questioningly, at him, her lower lip trembling. She didn't understand his action. Nothing like that had ever happened to her before and she interpreted it as rejection. Another possibility crossed her mind, then, but a quick glance at his wife, whose lush blonde beauty and obvious desirability gave the lie to that idea caused her to change her mind. *No! He couldn't be a gay one, at least I don't think so!* But there was a tiny doubt in her mind; she couldn't shake it, completely. Of course, sometimes even their wives don't know about them.

Finally, Artie's story was finished. The waitress brought their lunches. The food was delicious and they enjoyed it. Afterwards, they all had another drink, before venturing out for the afternoon.

While Zoe's husband paid the luncheon check and Lauren made for the Ladies' Lounge, Dave was alone with Zoe for the first time.

He leaned in close to her and hissed between clenched teeth, "Listen... I think you're damned attractive – sexy as hell, as a matter of fact – but I don't get why you're doing what you're doing right in front of that big gorilla of a husband of your's!"

Zoe smiled with relief. "Oh, you do like me then? I was afraid..."

"Afraid that I wouldn't?"

"Well... yes you didn't seem to react..."

"Did you expect me to do something stupid in front of your husband and my wife?"

"Not really. I just wanted you to know I..."

"You let me know one thing... Loud and clear, baby! You're a little cock-teaser... so lay off... unless you're serious!" Dave ground out at her.

"It'll be worth your while... if you want to meet me somewhere!" she promised.

"Like where?"

"On the ridge... up above the camp?"

"Out in the open... and take a chance on your husband finding us? Not on your life!"

"You don't understand about my husband. I'd have to have time to explain..."

"As much as I'd like to... sample your wares, Mrs. Berman... the fact is... there's too much risk... and I'm not willing to risk crossing that husband of yours!"

"Artie wouldn't do anything! As a matter of fact... he'd..." Zoe stopped. Lauren was coming toward them, and Artie was pocketing his change at the cashier's counter.

"He'd what?"

"They're coming – no time to tell you,

now, but will you meet me tonight, like I suggested?"

"I told you... the answer is no!"

Zoe was hurt. She'd never had a man turn down her offer to take him to bed, and she didn't know what to think or what to do. She decided to give up the pursuit! *Damn it, it's not worth it! I practically throw myself at him... and he tells me, 'No thank you... I'm not having any!' I wonder more and more maybe he is some kind of a closet queen!*

Her husband was there, big and jovial; he knew something had gone amiss. His suspicions were confirmed when Zoe looked up at him, her eyes miserable in defeat, and said, "Artie, darling, could I beg off for the rest of the day? I'm getting one of those sick headaches... and... I'd just be an awful wet blanket for everybody else..."

"Why, of course, Zoe, if you're not feeling right!" Artie sympathized.

"Oh, that's too bad, Zoe; you'll need some rest, so why don't we just call off the rest of our little tour?" Lauren suggested.

"Oh, no! There's no need for that," Artie said, trying to keep things together.

"I think that's best, too!" Dave added. "And, we sure do thank you for taking us around to see the sights."

"And thank you for the lunch, too!" Lauren added.

***

Artie Berman followed his wife inside their trailer. Closing and locking the door, he turned to her and asked, fiercely, "Well, what the hell happened?"

"He wasn't having any!" Zoe spat vehemently.

"You mean he turned you down flat?"

"Yeah, he seemed to think I was being too forward in front of you and his wife!"

"Maybe he's just being cautious."

"I suppose," she agreed. "He was afraid of being caught by you!"

"In other words, if I wasn't around he might not be scared off, is that it?"

"Maybe, but I got this crazy idea while I was talking to him that he might be..." She stopped, realizing she had no real basis for thinking of Dave Christie that way.

"What? What are you trying to say?" Artie prodded.

"Well, that he wasn't... all... man."

"You think he might be gay?" He was incredulous. "Kee-rist! I never thought of that!"

"Except... he did have a nice, big erection!" she told her husband, remembering how she had felt its throbbing heat in Dave's pants.

"Well, hell, then, what are you worried about?"

Zoe sat down on the edge of the bed.

"Well, he was almost prissy when he took my hand off of it, and told me not to touch him... unless I was serious."

"Unless you were serious?" Artie repeated. "I think you're wrong! He's interested, all right, but he's not taking any chances! After all I'm a pretty big guy, and he wouldn't want to tangle with me! You can't blame him for that, not many guys would be willing to! And maybe you came on too strong!"

Tears glistened in Zoe's expressive, gray eyes. "I-I'm not going to go through with it... Artie! I was practically throwing myself at him and he wouldn't have anything to-to do with me!"

"No! God damn it! I'm going to get into those tight hot pants! I want to fuck that Christie woman so bad I can taste it! Christ! It took every bit of will-power I've got to keep my hands off of her, waiting for you to score with that stupid son-of-a-bitch... and you know damned good and well that the way we work it, it's always a sure thing!"

"Except this time, Artie!" she flared. "And I don't want to get turned down again even for you! It makes me feel cheap... almost like I was out peddling it like some street whore!"

Then, it finally penetrated. Artie realized that his wife was really pretty upset, that she meant what she was saying. He softened, coming to sit beside her on the bed, his arms going around her, caressingly. "You know that isn't true, honey... and I'm sorry you feel that way about it! I'll make it up to you, you know I always do, and in the long run... everybody benefits! Hell! You like a strange lay just as much as I do!"

"Well, I bow out on this one!"

"After all the trouble I went to to set it up?"

"There'll be others!" she said, with finality, rising from the bed and shrugging off his embrace. "Right now, I feel like being alone. I think I'll go down to the village and shop around in those little tourist trap shops..."

"You won't change your mind... then?"

"No! It's made up!"

"Then I'll go after her on my own!" he threatened.

Zoe stared at him, not believing what she had heard. "But – our agreement?"

"You're breaking it by backing out!" he accused. "So think about it!"

"Damn you, Artie, you drive a hard bargain!"

"Then, you'd better reconsider."

"All right! I'll think about it... for a good long time! Maybe I'll think about it for three or four days until you get over that blonde or spot another you'd rather have! Then, I'll consider playing our little game, again!"

"You're being bitchy as hell!"

"Okay I *am* being bitchy... because I'm

upset... and I think I've got a right to be!" she defended. "And that's why I'm going shopping, to be alone, and maybe work it out of my system."

"All right... all right!" her husband conceded. "Just don't spend too much money on those junk curios. Okay?"

***

Hunter Mitchell had seen her first when she had gotten out of her car in the parking lot. The striking beauty of her jet-black hair... and the way she seemed to be poured into her capris attracted him... but when she had seemed to notice him, as he strode along toward the little delicatessen, giving him a smoky-eyed smile in passing, which caused him to stop and stare after her, her hips and buttocks doing provocative things inside those pants, he decided to get to know her better.

Billie Grant was with him. When she had finished picking out the foodstuffs they needed, he carried the bag of groceries outside and called Gavin Rust to him.

"Gavin... you take Billie on your hog... back to the camp and see she gets supper started!"

The other man looked startled, for a moment, his small, too-narrow eyes, regarding the tall, black-bearded leader,

Highway to Shame 91

calculatively, attempting to fathom what was going on.

"Right on Hunter!" he agreed, then asked, "What's happening?"

"I'm going to eyeball around, is all! Superboy and Dipstick can split with you, too!" He looked around, saw the two leather clad men talking to a couple of young, high-school age girls, obviously tourists and whistled them over.

The auburn-haired Billie had held her tongue, but now she asked, "Can't I go with you, Hunter?"

"No! You heard my orders, goddamn it!" He turned on her threateningly. "No... split!" He stalked away, angrily.

"What's happening, man?" Dipstick MacKay asked.

Gavin Rust filled him in.

MacKay was instantly angry, but he said nothing, asking only, "And he told you to ride Billie on your hog?"

"That's how he laid it on me!" Gavin told him.

"So let's split!"

The three men mounted their motorcycles. The food was in the saddlebags of Gavin's hog, and Billie was seated behind him. They swept out of the parking lot with a roar of engines. Dipstick MacKay brought up the rear.

Until two minutes before, he had been,

informally, the number two man; actually, it was he who should have led the group back to the camp, he who should have had the mama, Billie, up behind him on his hog. Now he was deposed, demoted by one of Hunter's whims. *Man! It's going to come to a head, now! It's got to be him or me!*

A mile along the road, MacKay dropped back, reducing his speed, constantly, until the others were some distance ahead of him, then, he pulled to a stop at the side of the road, dismounted and squatted beside his motorcycle. Soon, the other two men came roaring back. He pretended to tinker with the engine.

Gavin turned a wide U in the road and pulled alongside. "What's wrong?" he yelled.

"Carb's out of adjustment! You guy's go on back. I'll be there in a few minutes!" he lied.

"Need any help?"

"No! I can make it alone!"

"Right on!" Gavin agreed, let in his clutch and blazed on down the road, Bill following.

MacKay watched their departure. *Now... God damn it... I'm going to find out what that sonof-a-bitch is up to!* He remounted his motorcycle and headed back toward the village.

It hadn't taken Hunter but a few moments

to find her. She was poring over a table full of curios in one of the smaller shops. He stood in the doorway watching her for several seconds, before walking up beside her, boldly, and saying, "Hello, Miss... I'd like to return something you laid on me."

Zoe looked up, startled, into the black eyes and equally black beard of the leader of the motorcycle gang.

"Oh! Heavens! You scared me!" she gasped, then recovering her poise, she added, "It's Mrs.! Mrs. Artie Berman... but my friends call me Zoe..."

"I'm Hunter. Hunter Mitchell," he told her.

"You said something about returning something to me? I don't think I've lost anything, Mr. Mitchell!" she smiled.

"It isn't something you lost... I said it was something you laid on me!" he corrected.

"Oh? What in the world is that?"

"You smiled at me, a while ago, and not many people... that is... people like you, ever do that!" he explained. "So... I'd like to give one back to you..."

He smiled down at her, his white, even teeth gleaming through the blackness of his beard.

"Thank you, Mr. Mitchell!" Zoe thrilled. "You have a very nice smile!" Her grey eyes regarded him, warmly, the trace of interest sparking in them.

"Call me Hunter!" he said.

"Okay... Hunter it is!"

"And you're Zoe!" He looked down into her face, serious now. "You now have two choices..." he went on. "You can tell the dirty, no-good hog rider to get lost... split the scene... or secondly, you can accept my invitation for a drink!"

"You've got the most original line I've ever heard!" Zoe commented. "And, you don't sound like I thought you'd sound!"

"What do you mean?"

"Well. I thought you'd use all kinds of slang and rough talk, you know, like a tough guy..."

"I talk that way, too! I'm a college dropout... I'd be an engineer, now... if I'd stayed in school," he explained.

"And you want... to buy me a drink?"

"Yes... and the reason, of course... is I'd like to know you better... much better!" His smile bordered on lewdness.

Her heart jumped with excitement. She had never dreamed that she would actually meet this man. Yes! She had smiled at him, on purpose... hoping... but this was too much for her. He was really inviting her for a drink... with a sort of promise for further exciting things... Did she dare?

Yes! She did dare! The exhilaration of Hunter's open admiration for her... in contrast to Dave Christie's earlier rejection, did something for her female ego.

"All right!" she agreed. "I'll have one drink with you... if you really want me to!"

His eyes swept over her trim figure, from head to toe, liking what he saw and wondering: Does she dig what I want from her... or is she just a stupid, little cock-teaser? "That's what I want!" he told her. "And, I usually get what I want!"

She was startled for a moment. "Oh I see. Now you're the tough guy..."

"Yeah... that's it! Let's go!"

For an instant, she was frightened. He was so mercurial. One moment he was polite; the next he was a roughneck, and she doubted she should even go with him, now. There was no telling what might happen... what could develop. Artie's warning about not getting involved with this man came churning back into her mind. God! What if I get into something over my head... something I couldn't handle... like if he got violent... or something like that? She hesitated, shrinking away from him.

Firmly, he took hold of her arm, his smile charming, his voice well modulated. "Come on!" he grinned down at her, boyishly. "Let's go have that drink... and I'll let you go back to your square, establishment-type husband, who no doubt waves the flag, believes in the sanctity of God, mother... and Apple Pie!"

She giggled, nervously, and allowed herself

to be led from the curio store to a bar just three doors down. Their entrance drew stares and a rustle of comments among its tourist patrons. Hunter selected an empty booth near the rear of the bar and gave the order to a waitress, who appeared as soon as they were seated. He chose bourbon and water. Her drink was a martini.

"I probably shouldn't be doing this..." she offered, feeling somewhat guilty that she was doing it against Artie's orders.

"Your husband?"

"Yes... you described him to a Tee... a while ago!"

"And I suppose he also dislikes motorcycle bums... like me?"

"He's terribly prejudiced!"

"But you... what do you think?" he asked, serious, again.

"Well... I think you're terribly exciting!"

Their drinks arrived. Hunter paid for them, lifted his drink, toasted her, silently, and took a healthy swallow. Zoe sipped her martini and regarded his profile. *He is sort of handsome... a kind of wild, animal-like man... and there's a certain sexy thing about him... that almost makes me want to... to make some kind of play for him!*

But, she knew she wouldn't. It'd be breaking her promise... the agreement she had with Artie... and he'd told her, already, what he thought about an involvement with people like Hunter Mitchell.

"Is that all?" he asked, leering at her.

"Well... I'd also have to say that there's a certain wildness... about you... maybe untamed is a better word!" she said, thinking unconsciously about how he would be in bed, the sexy things he could do to a woman. to her! She raised her martini to her lips, again, taking a long drink of the gin, this time; then she attempted to change the subject. "Why don't you tell me... what it's like to live your kind of life?"

"What do you want to know?"

"Well... do you work? Are you married? Where do you live... when you're not out riding around on your motorcycles?"

"Slow down!" he grunted. "Let's take them one at a time!"

Hunter launched into a somewhat detailed answer, telling her he worked only when he needed money... no, he wasn't married, and motorcycles were a cheap form of transportation.

As he launched into other reasons for riding motorcycles, she stopped him to ask, "Isn't there a girl with you? Does she stay with you... all the time? What does she do?"

"Well... the girl's my mama sort of like a common-law wife!" he explained.

Her questions went on and on. Hunter answered. Their drinks were finished. He ordered another round... and finally another. Zoe was almost mesmerized by his talk, his animal magnetism, and as the alcohol befogged her brain, he became ever more fascinating to her. Dimly, she knew she was treading on dangerous ground. She was becoming sexually aroused – tempted, almost beyond reason – to offer herself to this magnificent, animal of a man. There was that delicious, pervading warmth in her loins, the wet readiness between her legs that caused her to cross and re-cross them, in an attempt to find a comfortable position. God! It'd be so exciting to be fucked by a man like this! She thought about Artie, for a moment. Hell! What Artie doesn't know won't hurt him! Before they had started swinging and joined the swap club, Artie had had a number of torrid affairs, operating under that same principle. Anyway he was threatening to go after that Christie woman on his own and leave me out of it completely, but I don't care now! Dave Christie was too chicken-hearted to take what I was offering him! Damn him! The more I think about it, the madder I get: the way he acted so offended when I was feeling his cock! Any other man would have been panting to fuck me, but oh no, not him! I still wonder...

She didn't have to wonder about Hunter. He was all man! His eyes devoured her. She knew that he, like most men, had been mentally undressing her, and she felt as though she had nothing more to hide from him. The raw desire for her was there in the hot salaciousness of his bold, unwavering stare, his open appreciation of her loveliness, but he had, so far, said nothing in the way of making a pass at her. He had, also, carefully refrained from touching her – yet she was hot for him. God! Dare she cross the invisible line of propriety to let him know what she was feeling, what she wanted?

Zoe had done it often, before, with several different men, just as she had with Dave Christie, but his man, Hunter Mitchell was different; , she knew his wildness could be dangerous. Artie's warning was still there, lodged somewhere in a far corner of her mind... but she ignored it.

Feeling only her sexual excitement of the moment, she turned her cool grey eyes on him. Her hand, below, silently reinforced the message, as her fingers lightly touched his thigh and inched their way toward his crotch, until they feather-brushed across the hardened shaft of his massive penis. She felt it throb warmly through the heavy denim of his jeans.

Hunter's dark eyes were flooded, instantly, with passionate desire. Damn! She's asking for it, plain as hell!

He grinned at her, lewdly, asking, "You like it, doll?"

"What? Oh! Please excuse me!" She was flustered. Quickly, she tried to withdraw her hand, but he was too fast for her. He caught her hand and held it close up against the pulsing bulk of his cock in his pants. "If you like it, then have a good feel, and after we'll go try it for size!" he leered, enjoying her discomfiture.

"No, please, Hunter, I-I don't know what made me do that! It was quite, er, accidental!"

"Accidental, hell!"

With his free hand, he picked up his drink and drained the glass. "Let's go!" he barked. His voice was hard as steel.

Then, keeping a tight grip on her arm, he walked her from the dimly lighted bar into the waning afternoon sunshine. Zoe was stunned by his sudden action, and she knew as they reached the outside that it was all a big mistake. She was out of her element with this roughneck.

"Let me go!" she hissed, unwilling to cause a scene that might attract attention. "You're hurting me!"

The motorcycle gang leader paid no attention to her pleadings, as he led her to his big motorcycle. "There's a nice spot up by the falls, out of the way with no people around! We'll go up there!"

"L-Listen! Listen to me Hunter! It's all a big mistake! I really don't want to go anywhere with you!"

They had reached his machine. "What?" He stared at her, disbelief on his face. "There's no mistake! You want to be fucked and I want to fuck you so that's what we'll do!"

"No! You don't understand! I-I didn't mean to... to..."

"The hell you didn't mean it!" he grated. "Unless you're just a little cock-teaser, and if there's anything I hate it's having some broad throw it around just for show and tell – and then try to cop out!"

Suddenly, Zoe jerked herself free of his strong grasp and ran toward her car. She was desperate, now! The man was dangerous! She had seen the smouldering madness in his eyes, and his swift change from amiability to raw, animal lust, mixed with his instant, flaming anger, frightened her.

Hunter could have caught her, easily but a struggle with her in public wasn't worth it.

The whole thing would be misunderstood, he could get arrested for assault... attempted kidnap and rape, and anything else that could be dreamed up. He looked after her, as she ran, like a frightened rabbit, to her car, got into it, started it and drove, rapidly, out of the parking lot. *Okay, baby doll! You asked for it, and by God, you're going to get it! Nobody plays cock-teaser with Hunter Mitchell, 'cos if they do, they pay for it!* He grinned, sardonically, to himself. *Damn! It'll be fun to take her off that high and mighty high horse she's riding! She'll squirm and wriggle before I'm through with her! Yes! God damn it! She'll squirm and wriggle on the end of my cock, and she'll just love it!*

Zoe's heart pounded in her chest! She looked back, briefly, to see Hunter Mitchell still standing beside his motorcycle and she was relieved that he wasn't following her. Oh, God! It was a horrible mistake! That man isn't normal, somehow, and there's no telling what he might do!

She drove fast. Getting back to Artie in their trailer was her only goal, at that instant, and she thought, miserably, about what her husband would say, if he ever found out! He'll never know about it if I can help it! Oh, God! I should never have done it, especially after Artie warned me! And, I hope and pray nothing else comes of this!

CHAPTER FIVE

The outing with the Bermans, Lauren decided, had been quite pleasant, but she was disturbed. She tried to tell herself it was just imagination, but Zoe Berman seemed to be almost too interested in Dave, almost like she was making a play for him!

Then, there was Artie, Zoe's husband. Why a couple of times I caught him looking at me like he was undressing me with his eyes! She felt flattered... that he was paying attention to her. But that look... ugh! It was vile! Like he wanted to... Lauren didn't want to finish the thought to its conclusion but she knew he was thinking about sex, with her as the sexual object. Her voyeuristic experience of the night before had been frightening, in a way; she had learned that, under the right circumstances, even she might change her mind, rearrange her attitudes and do something she'd be sorry for later, like wanting to have another man make love to her. She remembered with revulsion how she had reacted, what she had thought. If she could help it... nothing like that would ever really happen!

Driving the short distance back to their campsite, Artie and Zoe Berman had dropped them off at their camper, after Zoe had pleaded a sudden headache, which ended the day of sightseeing. She had accepted it. Maybe Dave'll take me out to dinner, anyway! It'd be nice, since we don't really go out often enough. She hoped it would put Dave in the mood, for later on, in bed...

As they entered their camper, waving goodbye, cheerily to the Bermans, Lauren asked, "Darling... can we still go out to dinner, tonight?"

"What? Dinner? Yeah... Okay!" He roused himself from his reverie long enough to give his wife the answer she wanted. *Christ! I'm one stupid son-of-a-bitch! She was practically offering it to me on a silver platter and I turned her down! There're ways, I suppose to carry on an affair. I should have tried to find out more of what she had in mind before I cut her off! Why, hell, a chance like that doesn't come along very often! And is she built! She's got a body that doesn't stop! Nice big breasts, good hips, a nice, tight, round ass! Damn it! I could kick myself for a crazy, stupid fool!*

Then, Lauren broke in on him, again. "I'm going to go take my shower, now while there's hardly anybody around!"

"Yeah... good idea! You go ahead..." he agreed. "I might do the same thing... a little later on!"

While Lauren went happily about the camper getting her things ready, Dave decided to take another look at the engine of the truck and while away a little time with some tinkering, since there was very little he could do as far as undoing the damage he had done to a developing relationship with Zoe Berman. *Of course, maybe she was just playing around, being a teaser, but the way she talked she was serious about it. but the thing I can't figure out is the why of it? Why me? She didn't know me from Adam!*

Dave went outside, walked to the front of the camper and opened the hood to the engine compartment. Idly, he looked inside, studying the engine, but not really seeing it. His mind was still racing. *But, if I ever get another chance like this I'll sure as hell take it! Sure! It'd be cheating on Lauren, but damn it, more and more there's nothing there for me! It's just not any fun! There's no charge! All she'll do is lie there telling me I can't do this or that! It's just a few kisses hop on and hop off, again! Christ, if she'd just let me play with her cunt... lick her clitoris... really get her ready for it... she'd have an orgasm every time! She seems to think anything but straight fucking is dirty and I get good and tired, trying to convince her otherwise! Hell, I'm getting to the point where I don't care whether I fuck her or not! I just can't get as excited as I should! She's got such a great body, but she won't use it for what it was designed for: for sex pleasure!*

He heard Lauren leave for the bath house. *Maybe... I'll try, again, tonight... to get her to go the oral route... put some zing back into our sex life! Come to think about it... there hasn't been much of it, lately!* He spotted a frayed wire leading to the headlights. Deciding that he ought to wrap it with some electrical tape, he went to the storage compartment in the side of the camper to get it.

Just then, he heard a car crunch by on

the park road, below the campsite. He looked up, recognized the car, instantly; it was the big Mercury station wagon they had been riding in earlier. Zoe Berman was driving... and she was alone! Dave made up his mind, right then! *Hell! Maybe there was something he could do after all! She's alone and probably going down to the village! It's only about a mile, and I could walk down there, maybe get to talk to her, find out what she's thinking! Hell, I might be able to get something going with her, besides I need the exercise, and the walk'll do me some good!*

Closing the hood of the truck, he went inside the camper, found a piece of paper and scribbled a note to Lauren, telling her he had gone for a walk down to the village.

With a spring in his step and a blithe whistle on his lips, Dave set off at a fairly brisk pace. *Damn, with a little luck...*

It was an invigorating walk; he enjoyed the clear, smog free air that pumped in and out of his lungs as he hiked along. Arriving at the rustic village, he spotted the Bermans' car in the parking lot, and in a very few minutes of poking around in the various stores and bars, he found Zoe. She was seated in a booth, at the rear of one of the bars, and she was with a black bearded, leather-clad motorcycle bum. *Well, I'll be damned!*

He sat on a stool at the bar and ordered

a beer. He drank it, slowly, glancing covertly at them and came to the conclusion that it was her own damned business what she did. And, I don't have any business interfering! She sure must be desperate, trying to get her kicks with a character like that!

Dave had intended to drink only one beer, but he ordered a second and drank it as he watched Artie Berman's wife giving her rapt attention to the bearded gang leader, for of course, he had recognized him as the one who had passed them on the road with a jeer, the day before, and who had flipped him the middle finger. Finishing off the second glass of beer, he left the bar. There's no point in sticking around here!

He stopped into-one of the rustic curio shops, bought some picture post cards and a scarf for Lauren, feeling he should bring something back for her... if only to prove he had actually visited the village. Then, carrying his small package, he headed back toward their campsite, the camper... and his wife.

Strolling along the road, in no particular hurry, he enjoyed the scenery. He was, perhaps, only a quarter mile from the camp, when he glanced back over his shoulder to see the Bermans' big Mercury station wagon approaching, rapidly. As the car came close, he saw Zoe's tense, frightened face. Hell! Something's wrong! He waved his arms at her, vigorously and shouted, "Stop! Hey... Zoe! Stop! How about a ride?"

Oh, it's Dave! Thank God! She brought the car to a squealing stop, glancing back down the road and seeing only Dave Christie dog-trotting up to her. She was still afraid that Hunter Mitchell might be following... somewhere behind.

He was at the side of the car, now; Zoe looked up at him, her frightened grey eyes the only spot of color in her white, fearful face.

"What's wrong... Zoe?"

"Oh, D-Dave... I'm scared! It's H-Hunter Mitchell! He... might be f-following me!"

"Why?" He looked back down the empty road.

"He... wanted to take me... up in the hills... s-somewhere on his motorcycle and..."

"And, what? Fuck you?"

She looked down, her face flushing, slightly, "Yes..." she trembled.

"What in the hell did you pick him up for then?"

Her eyes questioned.

"I saw you... in the bar with him!" he explained. "He seems like a damned poor choice!"

Dave saw that she was shaking, violently, and knew she was in no condition to be driving. "Slide over!" he said, firmly. "I'll drive you the rest of the way!"

She obeyed, and Dave opened the door and got into the driver's seat.

"I was angry... I guess..." Zoe tried to explain. "I was mad at A-Artie... and mad at you... too... for... for..."

"For turning you off during lunch?"

"Hell, what did you want me to do, grab you and lay you right there, in the restaurant?" he asked, exaggerating.

"N-No but we could have been alone, tonight and..."

"We'd have been taking a chance of your husband catching us!" he reminded her.

"No, it would have been all right, with Artie!"

"What do you mean?"

"I mean, h-he wouldn't do anything..."

Dave looked at her, questioningly, not understanding, so she went on, "He does what he wants... and I do what I want!"

"So you tried to pick me up?"

"Yes... b-but there's a reason!" She looked away, not wanting to tell him... yet; it was the wrong time. Looking back down the road, she saw nothing on it, and heaved a sigh of relief. Now, that she had Dave Christie alone... she might be able to carry on... from where she had left off, at lunch, when he had rejected her advances. She would know, in just a little while whether or not he was interested. "Why don't you drive around, for a while... maybe we can find a nice... private spot someplace... where we can talk..." she suggested.

"Or... fuck?" His boldness in making the further suggestion amazed her. It had just come rolling out of his mouth.

"Or... *both!*" Zoe told him, her heart leaping with excitement. Well! Maybe he's coming out of his shell!

Dave put the car in drive and released the emergency brake. He drove quite slowly. The road led past the two camping spaces, but there was no way he could avoid passing them. He'd just have to chance being seen, either by Lauren or Artie... but Artie – according to Zoe – was no longer any problem.

Passing his campsite, he saw nothing of his wife, Lauren. He sighed with relief, "Well... my wife didn't see us!"

Zoe smiled and slid across the seat close to him. Likewise, he passed the Bermans' trailer. Artie was nowhere to be seen.

"We're in the clear... now!" Zoe said in a conspiratorial tone, snuggling close against his shoulder, her hand dropping, eagerly, to his lap to feel the heated bulge of his growing erection.

"This's where we left off at lunch!" he remarked.

"When you... so-so forcefully took my hand away... damn it!"

"Well... we don't have to go over that, again!" Dave told her, shifting his position, slightly, in the seat, and allowing his thighs to spread a little more. *Hell... if she wants to play... I won't stop her, now!*

She knew what to do. His change of position was all the signal she needed. With deft, sure knowledge, she zipped down the fly of his pants, her hand squirming inside to find the hardening shaft of his cock. She brought it out into the cooling air of the late afternoon and gasped, involuntarily, as she saw and felt its far above average adequacy. He glanced down to see her small hand holding it. Her bold approach, the erotic change of having this strange woman diving into his pants like that, caused it to jerk, throbbingly, in her hand, and he thought: *Christ! If Lauren would only break loose with something like this... once in a while... it'd be a whole new ball game!*

Zoe was ecstatic. *Oh, it's going to be nice... after all! MMMmmmmmmm!* "Dave... darling... you surprised me! It's even bigger than I thought it was!"

"Yeah? Well I guess it's big enough... to get the job done!" He was flattered but felt he had to be self-effacing.

"I have to tell you this..." she breathed into his ear. "Do you know what I thought... when you took my hand off of it?"

"No... what?"

"I thought you might be gay... or something like that!"

"The hell you did!?" Dave snorted. "I'm far from that! Except for when I was a kid, experimenting around – you know just growing up – trying to find out what it was all about. I've never had any yen for that sort of thing, especially after I found out about girls... and cunts!"

"That's a relief!" she sighed. "I like my men to be, well, all man!"

"Hmm... can't you feel it there in your hand?"

"Oh, God, yes... and I can't wait to feel it shoved into my cunt!" Zoe murmured, leaning down across his lap, her lips coming down to kiss the blood-inflated head of his cock.

As her lips made moist contact with the red satin of the corona, Dave moaned with the intense pleasure of the sensations her mouth caused. Damn! She's really hot for it! And I haven't felt so hot and bothered... for a very long time!

Artie Berman spent his time lounging in a folding camp chair, listening to a portable radio and drinking beer. He had just stepped inside the trailer for another cold can of brew, when he saw his station wagon coming up the road, but when he came back out a moment later, fully expecting to see his wife, Zoe getting out of the car, he was totally surprised. I'll be damned! She went right on by!

Looking up the road, he saw the big Mercury. There were two people inside. Zoe was the passenger... and the driver was a man. He shaded his eyes to look closer and recognized the driver as Dave Christie. An instant grin of deep satisfaction creased his big face. Zoe came through after all... it looks like! Now... the fun begins!

He set the can of beer down on the table and hurried to the rear of the trailer. Opening the storage compartment he removed a folding bicycle, assembled it, went inside to get his binoculars and peddled, happily off in the direction his car had gone. There's one thing for sure: they can't go very far on this road!

It was only about a half-mile farther on that he found the station wagon pulled off the road. A high, steep slope to the right ruled out his quarry's going up there, so he searched to the left, in the stream bed. He spotted them with his binoculars. Dave and Zoe were just disappearing around a bend of the stream where they would be hidden from the road. Dave, Artie noted, was carrying a blanket. Well... they're going to do some serious fucking... I guess, from the looks of things! Got their arms around each other and everything – just like a couple of kids going off to tear off a piece of ass behind the barn!

Putting his binoculars back in the case, he fished his car keys out of his pocket, got into his car and eased it carefully back into the road, hoping that the roar of the falls, unseen around the next bend, would cover the sound of the car's motor. He swung the car around in the road and drove down to where he had left the bicycle. Putting the homely looking but functional vehicle in the back of the station wagon he drove, rapidly, down the road to the camping area. It won't be long now! Lauren Christie's going to be surprised to see me!

***

Luckily, there were few tourists, who took the little side trip to these particular falls. There had been no cars on the road, which pleased Dave, and the spot he selected, in the stream bed, could not be seen from the road. Across the stream was an unbroken wilderness. It was perfect. He spread the blanket on the sand and reached for Artie's wife, to kiss her for the first time.

She came into his arms, easily, lifting her mouth to his. Their lips welded and tongues became busy, searching and savoring, while hands roamed, to find hollows, curves and hard muscle. After a few moments, she twisted her head aside and murmured,

"Dave... darling... there's one thing I have to tell you... b-before it's too late!"

He released her and she sank down onto the blanket. Mystified, Dave sat down beside her, trying to take her into his arms, again. He was impatient. There had been too much talk, already, as far as he was concerned. Zoe shrugged his hands away. "No! Not yet! I'm serious. I have to tell you something before we can go any further!"

Visions of several things clicked through his mind: Disease? Physical malformation? Menstruation? Pregnancy? "Well... what the hell is it? Don't be so mysterious!"

"Do you remember I told you... that Artie and I do our own things?" she asked.

"Yeah... you said Artie didn't mind."

"That's only part of it!" she explained. "There's a little catch to it."

Dave's face creased in a frown. "A little catch, eh? Like how much is it? Is that what you mean? You're peddling it?" He reached for his wallet in his back pocket.

Zoe stared at him, aghast. "Dave!" she gasped. "That's absolutely disgusting! I'm not talking about money!" With a quick movement, she gathered herself and sprang to her feet. "Besides, it's insulting, and I'm leaving... now!"

Quickly, he caught her hand, pulled her down to him and smothered her in his arms, his lips finding hers, again, to kiss her hard and meaningfully. After a moment or two, she relaxed and began kissing him back.

Then, when he broke the kiss, he growled, "I'm sorry, Zoe, I misunderstood... but if it isn't that... what in the hell is it?"

"I guess we're even, on the misunderstanding, now," she smiled, somewhat sheepishly. "But what I'm talking about is a trade, me for you and your wife, Lauren, for Artie!"

It was Dave's turn to stare at her, disbelieving what he had heard. "Am I hearing you right?" he gulped. "Do you mean you're doing this... with me... so that your husband'll get a crack at Lauren?"

"Yes..."

"My God... I don't know... she's so..."

"So... what, Dave?"

"Well, hell... I might as well tell you! She's such a hidebound, puritan type... that I-I... haven't been much interested, lately... in having sex with her!" he explained.

"Then... you wouldn't have any objections?"

"Hell yes... I would! She's still my wife... and I do love her!"

"But you do want me... don't you?"

"Yes... but... I couldn't throw her to somebody else!"

"All you have to do is agree to let Artie operate his own way!"

"Give him a clear field... in other

words?"

"That's the idea... and she can make up her own mind... Okay?"

Dave tried to visualize his wife in another man's arms, being fucked by him. It was no use; the pictures wouldn't form in his mind, but he knew it would be an actuality if he accepted the terms of Zoe's offer. *It's a damned big decision! And, I can't see Lauren going along with it!*

Zoe's hands were busy on him, again, as she used her fingers to outline the bulge of his hard cock inside his pants. "Well, lover, have you made up your mind?" she asked.

"Yeah!" he grunted. "Come here! I want to fuck you!"

"Ooh, yes, Dave! I want you to, I want you to *fuck* me, *hard!* I want you to... tear me apart... with your big... hard *cock!*"

He knew he should have not been so hasty. Lauren had just been committed to a sexual encounter with Artie Berman without her knowledge or consent, because of his lust for the beautiful, black-haired wife of the other man. *But, damn it, let's face it... Lauren just doesn't do anything for me any more!*

Resolutely, he reached out to the clasps at the back of her halter top, unhooked them and helped her to shrug free of the skimpy garment. There was no bra underneath. The full, round orbs of her satin-smooth breasts were liberated to his fascinated gaze.

Instantly, he cupped the pliant flesh of them in his hands, kneading and massaging their magnificent springy firmness and rolling the hardening, luscious, pink nipples between his fingers. He felt them distend and throb to erection as he manipulated them to pointed cones of sensitive flesh.

Then, while he nuzzled, licked and kissed her breasts, Zoe undid the zipper at the side of her tight-fitting slacks. She knelt up, kicked off her sandals, and he helped her, pulling the stretch material of her capris down over the svelte curve of her hips and buttocks. She rid herself of the slacks and tossed them aside. Her panties followed, and she was naked. Dave drank in the beauty of her body for a moment, before he pulled her down beside him on the blanket. His mouth came down hard on her lips, his tongue stabbing deep into her mouth. She sucked at it, while his hands explored her body, moving down over the smoothness of her back to the rounded, resilient protuberances of her buttocks, where his fingers dug in, cruelly, as he kneaded the flesh of them through his fingers.

Her hands were certainly not idle. She reached, found and zipped, his fly coming open, then she unbuckled his belt, before her hand dipped in to liberate his massive, hard cock from his confining pants. She fondled it, feeling its great length and girth. It was warm and pulsing in her hand... and hard as granite, and she felt it throb to even greater erectile dimensions.

Gently, Zoe used her nails to scratch, lightly, up and down the hard length of his prick; then, she reached under to cup his sperm-bloated testicles, and she used her nails again to taunt them. She heard him gasp, involuntarily, his cock jerking in her light-fingered grasp, seeming to grow harder, yet, as she titillated him to vibrant readiness.

Using both hands, now, she grasped the shaft of his cock and gave it a powerful squeeze. Then she began to twist and wring, her hands going in opposite directions, as though she were expressing water from a rinsed garment. It was a deliciously erotic sensation that sent almost excruciating sexual excitement swarming through the length of his prick. It brought a short, sharp intake of breath from him, and a deep-throated moan was wrung, from his lips. Without warning he broke the deep, soul kiss and sprang, suddenly, to his feet, clawing at his clothes to get them off.

Zoe had to release his cock, as he jumped up to his feet, but she recovered it quickly, her mouth following her hands. She knelt before him, milking back the loose fold of his foreskin to reveal the purplish, blood-engorged cock-head, her lips seeking it to kiss and lick, her tongue swirling, maddeningly around it, as she teased and taunted it, expertly; meanwhile, Dave stripped off his shirt and vest and flung them, aside. Christ! He hadn't been this excited in a hell of a long time! Looking down, he saw her pink tongue licking at him... almost as a kid licks an ice cream cone. Then, he knew what he wanted!

"Suck it!" he breathed. "Suck my cock... first!"

Without hesitation, her lips quickly encompassed the silky-smooth corona, her tongue running in circles around the flanges, then flattening along the frenulum to suck like a nursing baby; finally, the sinuous tip of her tantalizing lingual member teased at the slitted head of his cock, trying to insinuate its agile tip into the tiny orifice. His prick throbbed, achingly, in her mouth, and instinctively, his hips began to undulate back and forth, and she began to absorb more and more of his ample length and breadth, her lips sliding down and down over the shaft of his cock, until more than half of it was moistly sheathed in the warmth of her working mouth and throat. Delightful sensations cascaded through him. It felt wild... and insane, in the extreme. God damn it! I've got to fuck her... now! He wanted to shove his cock into her squirming cunt... and fuck her until she couldn't walk straight!

"God! That's enough... now! Leave enough of it... for me to fuck you with!" he groaned, reaching down, under her arms to hoist her up to him. Reluctantly, she was forced to release his throbbing cock from her voracious mouth; then, with desperate speed, he dropped his pants to his ankles and stepped out of them. His shorts followed in a second. He kicked the clothing aside, carelessly, as he stood fully nude, now, before her. He grinned with quiet satisfaction, when Zoe's eyes locked onto the lancing, massive hardness of his prick.

"Do you like it?" he asked.

"Oh, yes... and to think... I almost missed out... altogether!"

Quickly, then, he gathered her into his arms, his hands going around her to the lush fullness of her globular buttocks, his fingers digging into them to feel their smooth, round pliancy. Pulling her in hard and close, he slipped the hard shaft of his cock in between her legs, parting the soft, dark hair ringing her cunt-slit and sawed it back and forth in the receptive flesh of her furrow. He could feel that she was very wet and the pulsing heat that her cunt generated. The hard tips of her nipples pushed against his chest as her arms went around him, her hands smoothing across the mascularity of his strong back, then dropping down to his waist and down

over the lithe suppleness of his trim, flat buttocks to pull him, likewise, hard into her loins, until their pubes were in solid contact and the head of his cock nestled, firmly, all the way between her legs and back against the tiny, crinkled orifice of her anus.

Standing together, there, observed only by the primal wilderness, they were, for now, the only man and the only woman – or the first man and first woman – as they danced the ritual dance of sex, their bodies undulating against each other, his big cock rubbing, maddeningly, against the sensitive bud of her clitoris, as she straddled the hardened rod of his more than adequate prick.

"You do want it... don't you?" Dave rasped, his throat dry. "You want me to... fuck you?"

"Oh, God... I can hardly wait... to get your cock in me! Fuck me! Fuck me... quick!" she moaned. "Before I go out of my mind!"

Dave released her. She sank down on the blanket, lowering herself to it to lie on her back, her beautifully tapered thighs splaying out, obscenely, to receive him, while her hands went to her own breasts to cup and fondle then slide down across her flat belly to massage the inside of her thighs, her hands finally framing the heated flesh of her cunt. He watched her for a moment, as her hips described tiny circles of desire under her, and her eyes were drawn, magnetically, to the spear of his hard cock, a smile of lewd anticipation spreading across her lovely face.

"I still don't believe it!" she gasped, then giggled, girlishly. "You know... when Artie told me... about you... I thought you'd be ordinary!" She held up her arms, invitingly.

"So now would you say that I'm extraordinary?" he asked lowering himself down between her thighs.

"Oh God yes! You've got plenty of extra!"

The moment his flesh touched her she shivered with sensual delight, her limbs trembling with ecstatic anticipation.

"I'm going to stuff you full of cock... now!" he grated.

"Please, lover! That's exactly what I want! I want it wild, and hard, and deep!"

Their mouths locked, tongues searched and tasted, and she rubbed her undulant body against him, raising her loins to him to find the hardened rod of his prick, but he was holding himself poised above her, not ready yet to plumb the depths of her cuntal passage. There was one other thing he wanted!

His mouth left hers and moved down, hungrily, over her neck and shoulders, kissing and licking as he went. Then, he paid homage to the magnificent hemispheres of her satiny, alabaster-white breasts, their coral-tipped nipples sensitively vibrant as he sucked and tongued them, which brought gasps of pleasure from her lips.

Then, his mouth moved down and away, and his body slithered downward over hers, his hands replacing his mouth on the tingling mounds of her sensitive breasts, kneading and massaging, his strong-fingered digging into their soft resiliency bringing her a mass of delightfully erotic sensations.

And, now... his lips were on her ribs, below her breasts... and moving... on down to the firmness of her gently curving belly, his tongue taunting and exploring the recess of her navel, briefly; then they were moving away, following the line of down on her abdomen, until they arrived at the almost jet-black triangle of pubic hair mounded there.

Sliding his hands underneath her smooth buttocks that undulated, lithely, against his palms, he lifted them up to him, his tongue darting out to explore the inner softness of her satiny tapered thighs.

Zoe's loins were, now, a seething whirlpool of rapturous expectation, as she anticipated the exquisite sensation of his tongue on and in her torrid cunt. It was almost as though her cunt was the vortex of that whirlpool... and he was being drawn down into it...

Without warning, his tongue shot out,

darting into the soft folds of her secret opening like a striking snake. Deep into the warm, liquid depths it went, sending a sharp, shivering spasm of uncontrolled ecstasy up through her spine. The electric sensations raced through her with the fury of lightning... savage and unconquered.

She moaned in ecstasy. "Oh, Dave... darling! That feels wonderful... absolutely fabulous!"

Unceasingly, he licked and sucked at her, pressuring up through the responsive flesh of her furrow to find and draw up her clitoris into his mouth. It came to full, throbbing erection under his sensuously tantalizing tongue. Now, Zoe had to have him inside her. She wanted that huge cock of his drubbing deep into her cunt, turning her inside out... splitting her in two... destroying her with its titanic power. She wanted to be subdued and subjugated by it! And, she wanted it now... with all her being! God! She had to have it... more than anything else in the world!

She pulled at his hair. Her eyes were closed. She was completely overpowered by the ecstasy coursing through her.

"Shove it in me!" she demanded. "Ram that big cock of yours into my fucking cunt and fuck me with it! *Fuck me!* Oh, God. Fuck me to *death* with it!"

Nothing mattered but this moment... this moment of sex! She felt as if she were nothing but an unfilled cunt... a cunt that throbbed and ached for satisfaction and fulfillment. She was Cunt; he was Cock! And there was only the lovely, swirling, exultantly exhilarating sensations of her vibrant, throbbing pussy, as it waited, impatiently, expectantly... for the entrance of his massively solid cock.

Dave's lean, muscular body squirmed up over her, wedging her thighs wide apart. The fleshy petals of her luscious pink flower were open to him, more than ready for his plunging entrance. Then, as he poised there, above her, her eyes misted with the power of her emotion, and she begged, "Oh... please... don't make me wait!"

Smoothly, then, he went into her, the great hardened shaft of his cock, with its bulbous, lust-inflated head, bursting into the resilient, moist portal of her cunt, suddenly... shatteringly. It spread the elastic, coraline walls of her vagina, as it raced full speed ahead, plunging far up into the seat of her being, nudging past her cervix, painfully, to lodge hard against the back wall of her warm, needful cuntal passage to bring her the long-awaited pleasure-pain she wanted... and needed.

Artie Berman' wife screamed under him. It was a long, drawn-out, scream of sensual rapture. Her mouth was open, her eyes glazed with passion and her thighs quivered, as she received him to the fullest. His cock was thrust to the hilt in her. His pubic bone crashed into hers, and below, his sperm-heavy balls smacked hard into the hairless crevice between the fully rounded orbs of her buttocks.

Then, he began to saw his cock in and out of her cunt, fucking her with feral energy, never stopping, always probing deeper and deeper, pinning her to the blanket, pressing her legs back farther and farther, his great, hardened prick screwing and fucking into her cunt like a monster reptile sent from the underworld to gorge itself on her flesh. He was like a man gone insane as he plundered her tender, clasping cunt.

Zoe pulled her thighs back until they mashed down hard against the tingling, swelling mounds of her large breasts, exposing the festive table of her loins to the feeding monster of his foraging cock. Her hips were undulant, rising in counterpoint to his hard, thrusting cock; together, they composed a great symphony of sexual desire, its soaring central theme one of torrid sensuality as they moved closer to the smashing finale.

Zoe's loins were a blazing furnace, the searing flames blotting out all rational thought, except those of pleasure, and she was aware only of the jabbing, thrusting, coupling of cock and cunt, below, and the slapping of flesh on flesh, which sounded loud in the forest stillness. She heard, also, the liquid sounds of the viscous lubricants of her vaginal walls as he pistoned in and out of her pulsating cuntal sheath.

Acutely, she was aware of his hands that ran over her body, their warmth on her sensate skin like licking flames over a hearth-log and his lips were on her mouth, her throat... her swollen breasts, sucking, licking and biting, his teeth nibbling at the erect buds of her nipples, until tiny rivulets of blood sprang from them to flood his mouth with the salty flavour of it. Her passion soared with the masochistic pleasure; it heightened the overpowering ecstasy of her desire-filled cunt, as his body covered her, the hot friction of him deliciously swarming against her, his hard-muscled body straining to bury the Herculean length of his cock to the very hilt in her pulsatingly lustful cunt with every downward plundering, goring thrust.

Then, they both heard it, distinctly, but at that moment, as they drove toward the rapture of sexual climax, they could not have stopped to find out what it was. It was the sound of thrashing brush, on the bank above them, as something – or someone – moved through the thick chaparral, rapidly, noisily. It could have been a frightened animal... a deer perhaps... or a horse that had wandered away from its corral... But, to the couple on the blanket, nothing mattered but the flaming passion that had caught them up in a boiling cauldron of molten steel, melding their flesh, blending them into one sensate being, aware only of the sensations of flaming rapture... of the imminent release for which they strove.

Dave Christie filled her. He filled her... and fulfilled her, completely; it was almost as though his rampaging cock was a missing, complementary part of herself... and she wished it could go on and on forever... just like this... being fucked and fucking back in wild abandon. God... *Oh, God!* If she could have only one wish it would be that... and she would be happy for the rest of her life... wanting or needing nothing else!

She gasped. Incoherent words came tumbling out of her mouth, as she panted for breath, her body reaching out to grasp the orgasm that was coming to her, bringing a release from the agony of waiting... from the overwhelming ecstasy of nerves too long supercharged with sex sensations.

"Screw me... Dave! Fuck me! Fuck me... forever... just like this! Oh, God... ram it in deeper. Ooooh! That's it! I-I'm just... about... ready... to... cum! Oh, God! I am! I'm *cuminggg! Aaaaaauuuuugggghhh!*"

Zoe writhed convulsively, under him, panting out her orgasm, as she soared to meet it and waves of body-relaxing, soul-satisfying release were hers to savor. She heard the wailing rasp of his breath, and she knew he would cum... soon.

His massive cock was a punishing, goring horn as it rampaged in and out of her with relentless fury. It made her whole body tingle, as she took him deep, up into her belly.

Feeling the scorching burn of his spunk as it was liberated from his sperm-laden balls, Dave suddenly stiffened above her. His back arched in one final, slamming thrust into the viscid moisture of her pulsing cuntal flesh. Then, he was spewing his semen far up into her vaginal sheath, his cock pumping wildly, while ecstatic sensations of relaxing euphoria swept over him, leaving him weak... and completely satisfied. He grunted his pleasure, as his prick continued to spasm, involuntarily, for a few moments; then he collapsed, dropping his weight full upon her, still cradled between her soft, beautiful, widespread thighs. He felt drained... figuratively as well as literally, after that final, frantic effort to satisfy her... and himself.

It was a dream. It was a heavenly vision of sexual fulfillment... and it was heaven, itself, to own such exquisite happiness... to know that it resided in your body... and that you could share it with another person... and Zoe reflected upon how lucky she was, how unbelievably glorious it was to enjoy sex to the fullest, with a real man like Dave! How wonderful it was. We're almost like Adam and Eve, or are Dave and I the King and Queen of sex? Out here by ourselves away from everybody, stark naked, in the wilds I'm the Queen of Cunt... and Dave's the King of Cock! She knew it was a fantasy, but a fantasy woven from the sexual satiety she felt.

Finally, after several moments, their breathing under control, now, their bodies relaxed, Zoe began, rhythmically, to squeeze the rapidly detumescent length of his cock, using the interior muscles of her still gently clasping vagina. It was an exquisitely sensual feeling for him... and for her. She did it several times.

Dave moaned, "God! That feels good! Do it some more!"

She did.

Again, hot blood rushed into the almost flaccid tube of his prick, and it became alertly erect and ready.

"Do you want me to fuck you... again... Zoe?" he asked, knowing that it was what he wanted, too.

"Oh, God... Yes, Dave, darling! And... don't stop! Don't let it ever stop!" she moaned, as his mouth welded to hers.

And, together, in the rapidly waning light of the late afternoon, they began, again to explore each other's bodies... to learn... to know... to give and to take, their pleasure coming to them in waves to their tingling, sensual bodies... and they forgot: each was married to someone else!

CHAPTER SIX

Thundering into the campsite on his motorcycle, Hunter Mitchell killed the engine and rocked the vehicle onto its stand. He sat still in the saddle and stared around the circle of quiet faces. The three men sat, hunkered down on their heels, holding tin plates full of a hearty stew, from which they had been eating. Dipstick MacKay looked back at him, a half-insolent smile curling his lips. It was a knowing smile and he would bide his time until the knowledge would work for him. Frank Superini, 'Superboy', gave a smile too, a broad one, his smooth, shiny face showing pinkly in the failing light. His hair was long, so blonde it was almost white, and he looked out through pale, blue eyes. He was boyish... almost feminine in appearance. It was a deceptive look. He was hard... tough... and virile.

Pluckily, Gavin Rust spoke up, "We didn't know when you'd show Hunter... so we started eating already!"

Billie was seated at the concrete camp table. She was already moving toward the stew pot on the fire to serve up a plate of stew for Hunter. They all knew that he was in a cold fury. Almost anything said or done, now, was liable to end in violence.

Getting off of his motorcycle, Hunter stalked toward the fire, only grunting an acknowledgement of Gavin's explanation. Silently, he accepted the plate of food from Billie and sat down, opposite her, his back to the others. He began to wolf down the stew.

After a few bites he said, "Dipstick... how come you split off from the bunch... and came back to the village?"

MacKay hadn't expected it. He was chewing a piece of meat, and his answer was low in coming. He shifted, uneasily, trying to swallow.

"Goddamn it, Dipstick, I asked you a question," Mitchell said, his voice cold.

The other man gulped and sputtered, "I just wanted to see what was keeping you... Thought maybe you got busted or something!"

"That's a lie! I saw you there! You were spying on me!" Hunter roared, whirling, quickly, and hurling the full plate of stew at Dipstick MacKay. It hit him square in the chest, spattering messily over his leather jacket.

"Christ!" MacKay yelled, as he lost his balance and fell backward. He clawed at his boot top for the razor-sharp can-opener he carried there.

Hunter reached him before he could rise, a well-aimed kick of his steel-shod boot sending the weapon spinning out of Dipstick's hand. His own switchblade was out, the long blade snicking out, dangerously. He menaced the fallen man, who was now holding his wrist and moaning in pain.

"Now... start laying it on me, you fuckin' son-of-a-bitch!" he snarled.

"I-I wanted to find out why you w-wanted to stay in the village."

"And did you?"

"Y-Yes... but, hey, like I-I didn't mean any... any harm!"

"You spill your guts to anybody?" Hunter spat out.

"No! No! I swear!"

"Make sure you don't! Because if you do, I'll hang you to a tree by your balls! Understand?"

"Yes!"

"And do you know who leads this group?"

"You..."

"Don't ever forget it... Dipstick! Just don't ever forget it, even for a minute!" he threatened, then relaxed, as he went on, "I ought to carve you up a little, but I'm not going to – yet! Your punishment's going to be to clean-up: washing pots; doing laundry; all that crap... understand?"

"That's Mama's work, goddamn it!"

"And that's what you do!"

MacKay was cowed. "Okay, okay... you win!"

The black-bearded leader stepped back and folded his switchblade knife. There was an audible relaxation of tension among the others, who had watched, fearfully, not knowing how far Hunter would go, or how violent he might become.

Billie had no idea of what had caused the trouble between the two men. She knew better than to ask. If Hunter wanted her to know... he would tell her; otherwise, there was nothing for her to do except keep her mouth shut. She moved toward the fire to ladle up another plate of stew for Hunter.

As the now undisputed leader regained his seat, leaving Dipstick MacKay groveling on the ground, in the mess of the stew Hunter had flung at him, he barked out, "Billie... let Dipstick do that!"

Seething in his humiliation, MacKay did the demeaning, servile task, spooning up a plate full of the food and placing it on the table before Hunter Mitchell.

Then, as he ate, he told them, "We've got a little project! There's that trailer up the way being pulled by a Mercury station wagon. We're going to watch them... and the first chance we get... we're all going to get that black-haired bitch and..."

"Gang bang her?!" Dipstick finished.

"Yeah, I might even let you in on it... if I don't slice off your cock and feed it to you... first!"

"Hunter! That's rape... maybe even kidnapping! You don't want to get busted for something like that!" It was Billie who burst in, emotionally.

"Who asked you?" Hunter grated, reaching across the table to slap her soundly. "You just stay out of this and keep your mouth shut. If you want to you can do what you want with the guy... after he's tied up... or maybe you'd like to make it with the broad?"

Billie's hand went to her face. It smarted from his slap. She didn't like his plan... but if she were to ride with Hunter... keep on being his mama... there was nothing she could do to stop him from carrying out his evil intentions.

"I'm sorry, Hunter..." she murmured.

"And just a reminder, Billie... that's the last time you try to interfere, understand?"

"Yes, Hunter." *God! That poor woman... whoever she is... They'll be like animals! At least... when all four of them make it with me... they don't mark me up... but a gang-bang like that... almost anything could happen!*

***

Feeling refreshed after her long, relaxing

shower, Lauren Christie returned to the camper to discover the note from Dave telling her he had gone down to the village. It didn't disturb her, particularly, but she did wonder, idly, what it was that had made him decide to go.

She went about her preparations for their evening out, together, putting on clean, dainty underthings, fixing her blonde hair, brushing it and fixing it, lightly, with a hair spray, then she applied make-up sparingly and tastefully to enhance her own natural beauty. She would wear that new mini sheath she had bought a month ago, she decided. It's lucky I packed it and brought it along... just in case we might go out for an evening of fun. But, it was the fun... afterward, she was thinking about... hoping she'd be able to coax her husband, Dave, out of his shell...

Deftly, she slipped into her dress and looked at herself, critically, in the long, narrow mirror.

Yes! Everything was perfect. She was ready far in advance but perhaps, they could go out a little early for a couple of cocktails before dinner, live it up a little, relax. Dave does get to feeling... amorous when he gets just enough to drink! If I can get just enough in him, without his actually getting drunk...

The heavy knock at the door of the camper startled her. She had heard the crunch of a car's tires, but had ignored it, thinking perhaps it was one of the Park Rangers on an inspection tour... Or, maybe somebody gave Dave a lift from the village.

Opening the door a crack, she looked out to see Artie Berman standing there big and blocky. She knew, instantly, that he was angry. He scowled up at her, grimly.

"May I come in, Lauren?" he asked, politely, enough. "I've got to talk to you!"

"Dave isn't here..." she said, somewhat reluctant to let him in... alone.

"I know that!" he spat. "That's what I'm here to talk to you about!"

"He's just down in the village... he should be back, pretty soon..." Lauren offered.

"No! He's not in the village! I just saw him... up by the falls! Now, can I come in... because you and I've got to talk... about what he's doing... and it's got to be private. I don't think you'd want anybody else to hear... what I'm going to tell you!"

Something in his words, the look on his face and the mysterious manner of his speaking alarmed her, and against her better judgment. Lauren opened the door to allow Artie Berman's huge figure to lumber into the small confines of the camper.

"Wh-What's Dave doing that's so... so mysterious or out of the ordinary?" she asked, adding, "Dave doesn't ever do anything wrong, or against the law..."

The big, barrel-chested man closed the

door behind him, with a bang. Turning on her, he spat, "What makes me so damned mad... is that they're both pulling the wool over our eyes, or they thought they were until I caught them... dead to rights!"

Lauren' eyes widened in further mystification. "What on earth are you talking about... and who are 'they'?"

"Your husband... and my wife that's who!" Artie gritted. "They're up in the canyon above, screwing like a couple of minks in heat!"

She gasped, not wanting to believe. "You m-mean... Dave... and Zoe... are... are?" Unable to finish, she collapsed onto the bench of the breakfast nook, her face in her hands. "I-I can't believe it!"

"I saw them – with my own eyes!" he held up the binocular case. "They were down in that stream... fucking like a couple of rutting animals!"

"N-No! No! Dave w-wouldn't?! It's not possible!"

"Well... I guess you don't know your husband, just like it seems that I don't know my wife, but it's a fact... and I want you to see for yourself!"

"I-I couldn't watch him!" she moaned, knowing that her heart would break if she actually had to watch her husband make love to another woman.

"That's beside the point!" Artie Berman

was grim. "But something's got to be done about them! They can't go around... behind our backs... fucking each other... without somebody paying the piper!"

"Oh, G-God!" Her mind visualized separation, divorce, lawyers asking probing questions, the judge sitting implacably... finally giving his decision... property divided... and she was glad of only one thing, as her mind raced, whiningly: *W-We... don't have a-any children... yet... Thank God!*

"So... come with me, goddamn it! You're going to see for yourself exactly what I saw and we can't waste any time getting there because they might be finished... the way they were going at it!" Artie growled.

Lauren, in her dazed state of mind, allowed Artie Berman to put her in his car. She knew it was something she didn't really want to do. Nothing could be gained... but there was that inkling of doubt... that necessity to see for herself... not that she disbelieved Artie – the man seemed to be so sincere, concerned... agitated at his wife's behavior – but if she did see it... it would dispel her indecision. She would be in a better position to make a judgment... like Saint Thomas, who had to be shown... first.

Rapidly, Artie Berman drove up the road to the spot where he had found his car parked earlier. He pulled the car off the road, helped Lauren out, then holding her hand, he struck off through the brush, to the left of the road, above the stream bed. Lauren shrank back, complaining, "The underbrush'll ruin my clothes!"

"Hell... that's not important... compared to what else is being ruined... by them!" He pulled her roughly along, behind him. "It's only a little ways... anyway!"

True to his word, after they had gone less than fifty yards through the underbrush, they came to the tree-line on the bank, above the stream. Artie used his binoculars to scan the area. Dave and Lauren were below on the sand a little further downstream than he had thought they would be. It was a perfect scene!

"Here!" he grunted, handing Lauren the high-powered glasses. "Just step up on this log... and take a look... right down there... to the left!" He pointed out the spot.

Her trembling hands accepted the binoculars, and she trained them on the prone figures, below. She couldn't control her involuntary gasp. It was Dave... and Zoe Berman lay on her back, legs splayed, obscenely, as she cradled Lauren' husband between them, his hips rising and falling, rhythmically, driving his hardened penis deep into her vaginal passage.

Quietly smiling to himself, Artie watched as the expressions on her face changed from disbelief to acceptance of the fact... followed by helpless anger... and despair.

"Believe it, now?" he chortled. "Those glasses put you right down there, don't they? To where you can actually see that big cock of your husband's going right up Zoe's tight, greedy cunt... "

Lauren was annoyed by his language, but she held her tongue from comment, answering, shakily, "Y-Yes... I can see... everything... real clear!"

"Take a good, long look... Lauren! You'll want to remember exactly what you're seeing!"

"I-I've seen... enough!" she mumbled, handing the glasses back to Artie Berman. She stepped down off the log and sat down on it numbly. *I'll remember it! I'll remember this... for the rest of my life! But, I can't believe it... or understand it! Why would Dave want to make love? No! Why would he want to... fuck... another woman like that? Fuck's the right word because he's doing it like an animal... out here in the wilderness... just the way Artie described it.*

The thing she couldn't really understand was why Dave had been avoiding making love to her... but was doing it with such obvious relish with Zoe Berman. Why? Oh, why? Tears glistened in her deep, china-blue eyes. There was an aching, empty hollowness in her... where her loving heart used to be. It wasn't true, she decided, that people's hearts were broken: they were just crushed and strangled, inside until there was nothing left... but a great, empty void of nothingness.

Suddenly, she leaped to her feet and ran, blindly, through the underbrush, the way they had come. The branches caught at her clothing, ripping her dress, snagging her stockings, as well as tearing, cruelly, at her flesh, lashing her legs and arms, searing her body with deep scratches.

"What the hell!" Artie plunged after her and caught her within ten yards. He held her struggling body close in his arms. "Take it easy... damn it! You'll hurt yourself!"

His big hands stroked her body, caressingly, and he crooned to her, "It's not worth it... to go tearing through the brush that way. It won't solve anything! We'll go have a drink together... and do some thinking about what we want to do next!"

She sobbed against his shoulder, inconsolably, for a few moments, as he continued to knead and massage the lush contours of her beautifully formed body, barely able to control his lust for her. Damn! I'd like to lay her down and screw her... right here... but this isn't the right place... or the right time, yet!

Finally, the first storm of her emotional upheaval was past. She dried her eyes against his shirt and said, "Please... take m-me... back, now!"

Still dazed... and definitely not thinking straight, yet, Lauren followed the big man back to his car and got into it. He drove straight back to his trailer, leading her, unresistingly, inside and fixing a strong, double bourbon and water for her. She gulped a quarter of it down, quickly. It calmed her. All of her emotion had been expended, for the moment, leaving a smouldering anger.

"Damn him!" she breathed, finally, choosing the only word that expressed her feelings exactly. "And damn her... for leading him into it!" She was remembering: This morning, Zoe was paying an awful lot of attention to Dave rubbing up against him... posing for him and doing all the things a woman would do to hook a man! And... he finally fell for it! She slugged down another big gulp of the whiskey.

"I don't know... about you!" Artie said. "But I feel they've played a miserable trick on us... and it'd serve them right... if we gave them tit for tat!"

"What do you mean by that?" Lauren was wary. She had been feeling ill at ease ever since Artie had held her close. She had felt the warmth of his loins against hers and the throbbing of a growing bulge in his pants. My God! He was getting an erection! At a time like this! And, the way his hands were roaming around means h-he wants m-me, wants to d-do the same thing! She knew the answer... already!

Artie lounged, easily, took a healthy swallow of his drink and smiled, lewdly, at her, "Well... my wife... and your husband are out there fucking hell out of each other... and I'd like to pay them off... an eye for an eye, a tooth for a tooth... and a fuck for a fuck! That'd make us even!"

"That's a... c-crazy idea!" she flared, full of indignation at his suggestion. "I'd never do that!"

"No... but Dave's doing it! What's fair for the gander... is fair for the goose... isn't it?"

It was preposterous... but suddenly, Lauren knew that watching Dave and Artie Berman' wife, Zoe, there in the stream bed had worked on her, insidiously. The glowing warmth in her loins warned her of mounting sexual arousal. She was more sure of it, when she realized that there was a copious amount of exuded moisture... down there... between the petals of her vaginal opening. Somehow, her concentrated thinking about trying to lure her husband to bed... then seeing him, through the binoculars fucking Artie's wife, which caused her so much pain and anger, subtly, almost insidiously, to produce a sexual need in her... a need that was increasing with every passing moment. Desperately, she tried to deny it. No! I won't! I won't give in... to myself... or him! It's wrong... even if

Dave is cheating on me!

Firmly, she set her glass down, rose and said, "But that's not for me! I'm still married to S-Dave... and as long as I am... I'll never do that!"

Artie Berman was on his feet, instantly; he was furious, his green eyes blazed, as he ground out, "You stupid, little bitch! I'm offering you a way of getting even... but whether you like it or not... I'm going to take out mine with you! No son-of-a-bitch can take what's mine... and not have to pay for it! Remember... that's my wife... lying out there, under your husband... while he fucks her silly!"

Lauren was genuinely frightened. Her face drained of color, and she turned to stumble toward the door of the trailer, a strangled, "No-No! Oh, God, no!" coming from deep in her being.

Suddenly, swiftly, Artie took her into his brawny arms, capturing her mouth with his own, his lips engulfing hers, completely and his moist, hot tongue snaked out to lash between her lips and teeth to kiss her deeply.

She resisted, attempting to turn her head aside and setting her jaw, but he brought his hand up to her face, his strong fingers pressing, cruelly, into her jaw muscles to force her mouth open. His tongue thrust in, hungrily, to probe and taste.

Disgust and revulsion rose in her, now, at the vile, intimately personal contact, and she struggled to escape from his encircling arms. It was futile. He was too big... too strong. He held her close, his hot hands moving, restlessly over the smooth female curves of her body, kneading and massaging the full-mounded protuberances of her buttocks, his great strength forcing her loins tight up against his, where the throbbing bulge of his erect penis pressed hard into her soft flesh. There could be no doubt about what he wanted!

Pulling her face away from his voracious lips, finally, with tremendous effort and struggling to escape from his imprisoning arms with all her lithe strength, she shouted, "Let me g-go! I-I'll never go to... b-bed... with you... damn you!"

"So! You're going to be a little tigress eh? Well... that's just the way I like them wild... and hot!"

"Y-You're trying... t-to force m-me and that's rape!" Lauren accused.

"You can call it that... if you want to... but you're going to get fucked... and you'll love every minute of it!" the big man chortled, lewdly. "As a matter of fact... you'll be begging me to fuck you!"

"I'll scream! I'll call for h-help!" she threatened.

"If you let out one little peep... I'll clobber

you!" Artie countered, showing her his huge fist.

She groaned in her futility, the sound coming from the very depths of her soul. She was trapped... and there was nothing she could do to escape this huge man, who was bent on a sadistic revenge. She slumped, weakly, against him, conscious that her own body was entrapping her, also, to keep her here. His penis pulsed against the softness of her belly, warmly... and unwanted, salacious sensations began to spark in her. It was all so confusing. She wanted to maintain her moral standards on the one hand... but the lubricious demands of her body were trying to gain the upper hand. It would be so easy to cave in... let her resolve go hang... and let happen what may... Maybe it'd serve Dave right... to let him know that I'd evened the score by... by letting Zoe's husband... f-fuck m-me! Her mind wandered to the sex scene she had heard and witnessed, accidentally, and she knew it could happen... Her thoughts had been so confused... but she distinctly recalled how she had wished, fervently, at that moment... that she could have been that girl on the sleeping bag... taking that bearded man's cock deep into her pulsing cunt... It could happen... even to her! Should she let it happen... or should she struggle against it? Oh, God! I-I don't think I could d-do it... and be able to live with myself... afterward!

When she relaxed her body against him, Artie Berman thought she had given up... that she was going to go along with his idea of getting even... and he misinterpreted her moan of anguish as one of intense feeling.

"You won't be sorry..." he crooned into her ear, walking her backward toward the big, double bunk at the rear of the trailer, kissing her, now, on her neck, his tongue laving the smooth, young skin, moistly, then moving up to poke into her ear, the tip of it running around the edges, tantalizingly. She couldn't help the little erotic shiver that shuddered through her body.

Pushing her down onto the built-in bed, he leered down at her and hissed, "You're a luscious, little thing... cute as a bug's ear... and twice as sexy!" He stretched his bulky body out on the bunk beside her, his hand roaming down across her flat belly, on down the outside of her lovely, tapering thigh, to the hem of her dress, then back up the smooth, warm flesh of the inside of her trembling thighs to the acute angle between them, pulling the dress up, at the same time, to expose the satiny white expanse of her flesh above her stockings.

Lustfully, he gazed down at her loins, as his hand kneaded her pubic mound through her sheer panties. He grinned his satisfaction and wormed a finger under the leg-band to insert it, smoothly, into the top of her quivering cuntal slit, then searched for and found the tiny bud of her clitoris, hidden in its protected valley. With gentle fingers, he rubbed at it and felt it surge to alert erection under his teasing manipulation. He knew the effect it would have on her. It was the seat of her sensuality he taunted.

Lauren felt the erotic thrill of his touch, but she cringed, inwardly, as she continued her unproductive debate with herself. Of one thing she was sure: She didn't want him to go any further, God! Why have I let him get this far? This is insane!

"Oh, please... Artie! Don't do-do that! I can't let you go through with it!" she moaned, as she felt his strong hands force her thighs apart. His hand was tugging at the thin, nylon crotch of her panties... the only protection there was for her defensively cringing vaginal opening.

"It's too late... baby doll!" Artie laughed.

Twisting his hand into the wisp of nylon, he gave a hard yank and tore the crotchband asunder, the material ripping, loudly leaving her young, tender cunt naked and defenseless. Her body trembled with the outrage.

"No! Oh, God! No!" she cried aloud, clenching her thighs tightly together, and a hand went down, instinctively, to cover her exposed shame.

"Take your hand away... and open those

thighs!" he ordered. "Or do you want me to get tough with you?"

"Y-You wouldn't dare... hit me!" she challenged.

Wild fury was in Artie's eyes. He shook his fist in front of her face. "Don't try me!" he threatened.

Disgust for herself, fear of Artie... and that need she tried to deny worked to defeat her. Slowly, she relaxed the quivering muscles of her thighs, allowing the alabaster-white, tapering columns to splay out, slightly, revealing the coral-pink furrow glistening moistly there, a sparse ring of golden, blonde hair accenting the loveliness of the spectacle displayed to his lewdly staring eyes, and he could see the soft pink of her inner petals, bedewed with viscous moisture, peeping out, almost shyly. Above, her clitoris pulsated, wildly, in its only half-hidden valley.

Then, it began for her!

She didn't want it... and she was helpless to stop it! Erotically, she felt his finger tracing the thin, pink slit of her pulsing, naked cunt, and she shivered with abhorrence, trying to squirm away from it. Then, he insinuated his finger into her cuntal passage, and there was a moment of salaciously prurient agitation... of warm need... and a strange, masochistic desire... of wanting it to go on, debasing her, humiliating her, beyond reason. She couldn't have explained it. It was just there...

keening in her body-mind, as he shoved that tantalizing finger deeper inside her warm, moist, trembling cunt.

Lauren moaned in an agony of emotional conflict of wanting... and not wanting. Her nerve endings were alive with the singing shimmer of sensual sensation, the electric shock of it spreading down her thighs and up her tingling spine. Her loins were responding to him in little surges. She didn't want it to happen this way... the way he had promised. *God! Why doesn't he just crawl on top of me, shove it in and do it?*

Screwing her hips down into the soft mattress, she tired to squirm away from his tantalizing finger, her moan changing to a mewling whimper of helplessness, as he thrust in and out of her several times, then he parted the softly curling blonde hair to make another, sudden, electrifying contact with the tiny, throbbing head of her erectile clitoris. She could feel the viscid moisture seeping from her, as unwanted and forbidden sexual excitement claimed her. With a groan, she clenched her teeth, fighting against the rising pleasure he was causing her. It was a last ditch battle. She knew she couldn't let it go on. *I'm being stupid... playing right into his hands... doing what he wants me to do!*

Forcefully, Lauren pushed against his chest, writhing and kicking to escape him. It was her last chance to get out of that trailer... without compromising herself!

"Stop it! Leave me alone damn you!" she hissed. "You're just using me f-for your own purpose!"

Her sudden change of mind and the force of her attack caught Artie Berman off guard, but he wasn't surprised enough to release her. He caught her wrists in his steel-fingered grip and pinned her to the mattress with his bulky body.

"You little bitch!" he grunted, forcing a beefy thigh between her legs to wedge them open, while his finger went right on plundering the moist readiness of her clasping vaginal opening. "You're just as hot for it as I am! Your cunt's all wet... ready to be fucked... but you won't admit it! So... why don't you relax... and start to enjoy it?"

She stared up into the lewd smile on his face, no ready answer coming to her. Oh, God... he's right!

Then, slowly, Lauren stopped struggling, and she relaxed down into the softness of the mattress, the insane horror of her situation drumming into her frantic brain. She had been trapped... and part of the snare had been her own body.

Tears of humiliation began to glisten in her eyes. She was revulsed by her own role, but now there was nothing she could do, as she found that the teasingly cruel play of his fingers in her cunt seemed to elicit uncontrollable responses in her. Against her will, she felt her hips begin to undulate in tiny, lascivious circles.

Rolling her head from side to side, the maddening sensations in her building ever higher, she realized that she was no longer trying to escape him. Her hips were beginning to raise her loins up to his plundering hand, wanting more of the frenzied, nerve shocking sensations that vibrated through her tender, sensate pussy.

"Oh! OOoohh! *OOOooohhh... God!*" she whimpered, involuntarily.

Artie released her wrists and bringing a hand up, stopped her flailing head, grabbing a handful of her hair to hold her tight. He kissed her, solidly, his tongue sliding shockingly deep into her mouth, while below he continued to massage her naked, defenseless cunt. After a few moments, he mumbled into her mouth, "It's time to get those damned clothes off!"

Dully, she knew she would need to get undressed; it was almost a foregone conclusion. He had already ripped her panties away. There wasn't really much left...

Lauren felt him raise her up, heard the zipper of her dress whisper down her back... and she closed her eyes. She didn't want to think about what she was doing.

Helping him with the proper movements, at the right time, shrugging her shoulders, raising and lowering her hips, she was soon wearing only her bra and the remnants of her panties, then as he unfastened her bra, she felt the cool air rush over her swelling breasts. He could feel the contrast of her hard, erect nipples brushing his palms as his work-hardened hands encompassed her smooth, springy tit-flesh to knead, caress and massage. Then, he was teasing the maddeningly sensitive nipples, rolling them between his fingers to generate even more sensation in her.

Finally, she felt his wet, hot mouth as he took one of the erect, sensitive buds, including the whole areola, between his lips, his tongue licking and lips sucking hard on the extruding nipple. It was maddening... and huge blinding streaks of heat lightning grounded in her loins. Now, she was moaning almost unceasingly.

Artie paid the other breast similar homage, his long, agile tongue trailing, wetly, down through the narrow defile between the magnificent orbs of her breasts. Lauren found herself tensing her stomach muscles, as he slithered down over her body, tongue darting wetly into the dimple of her navel, while his hands still continued their constant caressing of her lusty breasts.

Now, she could feel his hands leave her naked bosom to move down along her ribs and the outside of her thighs, catching the waistband of her ruined panties and removing the wisp of ragged cloth; next they massaged up the insides of her satiny-smooth thighs, spreading them wide to completely expose her naked pussy to his view. The sound of his raspy breathing was loud inside the trailer, as once again, his fingers plundered her tight, wet cuntal passage... but this time he had plunged not one, but two of his fingers deeply into her heated vaginal portal. Then, suddenly, he was gone. She kept her eyes closed. She guessed what was happening and knew she was right when she heard the sigh of a zipper, the rustling whisper of cloth and the thump of his shoes on the floor. She kept her eyes closed, because she didn't want to look.

"You can't keep your eyes closed all the time, Lauren, so you might as well open them up and take a good look!" he grunted.

It was true! She'd have to look at him sooner or later. Slowly, reluctantly, she unclenched her tightly closed eyelids. She saw him... saw it... and gasped.

He was naked, kneeling between her widespread legs, his big face distorted in a lewd grin, as he watched her reaction. Her eyes swept over the hairy bulk of his big, solid body, her gaze inevitably coming to rest, and locking on to, the thick length of his fully erect penis. It lanced out obscenely from his muscular loins below. His hands went around the hardened shaft to stroke its massive length; with each stroke the foreskin slipped easily over a bulbous, blood-inflated cock's head that glistened with precum. She could see it throbbing and jerking in his hand like some wild animal searching its prey.

"How do you like it?" he chuckled. "Pretty nice... isn't it?"

Lauren could only stare in miserable humiliation. She felt degraded at the sight of her own naked, obscenely spread body... waiting to be taken, sexually, by this man who was not her husband. Filled with shame, she had never felt more helpless in her life, not least because of those waves of unwanted desire that flooded through her being, bringing feelings of utter depravity and surrender. Then, as she watched Artie stroking himself... she realized the enormity of it. *It's bigger than Dave's! God! How can I ever... t-take all of that... up inside of m-me?*

Seeing her horrified stare at his outsized cock, he told her, "When I get this cock of mine in your tight little cunt, you'll know you've been fucked... but good! You'll be climbing the walls... prick-hungry and wanting more of it!"

She hardly noticed his filthy language anymore. Her mind was too involved with the hopelessness of her position. He was going to fuck her... ravish her helpless body, and she couldn't stop it; indeed the worst part of it was that she didn't want to stop it!

Leaning forward, suddenly, Artie dropped the full weight of his bear-like body on top of her, knocking the breath from her lungs for a moment, the long, hard thickness of his cock pulsating against the soft flesh of her abdomen, while his avid hands, once more, squeezed and dug into the smoothly mounded fullness of her breasts, savagely, causing her to whimper in pleasure-pain beneath him. His mouth sought hers, voraciously, and his tongue stabbed deep into her mouth and throat, as animal sounds of pure lust came from deep in his throat.

She lay under him, petrified, accepting his painful caresses and brutal kiss... but she was afraid; the moment was close at hand... when he would be shoving that monster cock deep inside her.

After a few moments, he realized her inaction... her lack of further response to him. I'll fix her... damn it! He knelt up, between her legs, grasped her legs just under the knees and spread her thighs wide, then moving forward, as far as possible, he settled back on his haunches, his cock's head just grazing the vivid pink flesh of her cuntal furrow.

He dipped a finger into the thick juices of her vaginal opening and spread it on the pulsing head of his cock, then deliberately, he slid it up the sensitive groove formed by her inner labia, the bulbous head pressuring through it to slip easily onto the tiny erect bud of her clitoris. He moved slowly, delicately, knowing that it would generate intense sensations... so erotically powerful she wouldn't be able to resist.

Her body responded tremulously, instinctively, her loins rising to meet the rubbery glans, as he sawed it back and forth, lightly, up and down the short length of her achingly sensitive clitoris. Firmly, he held her thighs open while he teased at her pulsing, vibrant slit.

Lauren began to moan under him, and her head began to flail from side to side, again. Her face was distorted with building passion.

Then, when she was sure that he must be ready to plunge his monster cock into her, he ceased the tormenting agitation... but it was only for a moment. Now, still haunched down between her legs, he was using his hands on her pussy. She felt him place his thumbs against the soft, trembling inner lips of her cunt and draw them slowly apart, exposing her flushed vaginal passage to his hungry gaze. Damn! She's really nice and tight!

Holding her trembling cunt-lips spread apart, he shoved his hips up until the head of his cock, blood-engorged and shiny red, made electric contact with the tender, pink flesh of her vaginal passage. He didn't try to enter her. He just moved slowly back and forth, the very tip, only, going into her, teasingly, steadily.

"Oh! Oooohh! God!" she moaned, uncontrollably, as her hips ground up at him, in an attempt, now, to capture his tormenting cock. *He's teasing m-me! Oh, God! I've got to... have it... inside m-me... now!* She could no longer deny the reality of her need.

Artie watched her lovely, contorted face, as he continued to tantalize her wild, searingly hot cuntal opening with the head of his cock, satisfied that she was losing the battle with him... and with herself.

Quickly, then, he shifted his position, coming down over her, his hips wedged in the angle of her thighs, his loins poised over her with his cock still working in the juices of her open-petalled cunt. He held himself aloft on brawny arms, still allowing only the head of his cock to stimulate her. Now, he began sawing up and down the length of her palpitating furrow, starting at the top, his bulbous cock's head pressuring down through it, to rub her clitoris, tormentingly, on down to the mouth of her cunt where only a mere half-inch of the head tantalized the opening. He felt her countering hip-thrusts up against him, but he never allowed her to capture him, as he moved up high, again, to repeat the process almost endlessly.

God! It was such torment. He just hung there, above her, teasing her and Artie waited, patiently, for her to break.

It had gone on so long! She wanted him... needed him, now... and he was playing games with her... a cat and mouse game of his own making. Suddenly, she cried out, from the depths of her soul. Her decision had been made for her... her traitorous body demanded it. She wanted to be fucked... now!

"Artie! Make love to me! Put it in... and... and *do it!*" Lauren wailed.

He grinned with lewd satisfaction. This's it! Damn it! She's really ready to be fucked now! Hot as a two-dollar pistol!

"You can do better than that, baby!" he told her.

Lauren Christie looked up at him, imploringly. She didn't understand him... didn't know what he wanted. "B-Better?"

"Yeah... you want it... you ask for it... with the right words!" he grunted, not letting up for an instant, as he used his cock-head to stimulate her beyond reason.

"N-No! I c-can't say those awful things!" she countered.

"You do know the words, though?"

God! Yes... I do know them! I've heard them so often! And I've even thought them... but...

"Y-Yes..." *But... I can't I just can't say them out loud!*

"Then, start asking me to fuck you!" he demanded.

"No!"

"Okay! I'll stop... right now... and you can finger-fuck yourself!" he threatened.

"Oh... *please?*"

With an effort of will, on his part, Artie stopped and hung, motionless over her. He was bluffing her. Just as he bunched his muscles to drive his giant cock into her, anyway, she changed her mind. Her hands went up and around him to his meaty buttocks and hauled him back down to her.

"F-Fuck me... Artie! Oh, please... fuck me!" she moaned, her pelvis straining up to him, yearningly.

"Now... you're on the right track!" he chuckled, barely able to hide his elation. "Go on! What with... God damn it?"

"Your cock!" she spat, her voice low with angry need. *"Fuck me... with your big, stiff... cock!"*

"Where?"

"In... my cunt!" she growled.

"How?"

"Hard... and deep!" Lauren couldn't believe that it was she who spat out the vile obscenities. He made no attempt to do as she begged, and she growled, "What m-more... do I have to say... or do... to get your cock in me... f-fucking me?"

"Just take my cock in your hot, little hand and put it in that cute cunt... for me!" he ordered.

God! He just keeps dragging me down farther and farther! Making me beg for it and now... ordering me to put it in m-myself! She flared out at him, "No! I-I won't do it! Haven't you done enough t-to me... already?"

Yet, against her will, her small hand went down to between them, reaching for the Herculean shaft of his cock... but stopping short of actually taking it in her hand. It was too much! She couldn't bring herself to do it. He had humiliated her and degraded her... almost to the limit of her tolerance.

"Do it you little bitch!" he grated, an animal snarl in his voice. "Put my cock in... now... or you'll be left high and dry!"

Reaching the final inch, she grasped but couldn't encircle his massive thick, lust-inflated cock. She felt its true size for the first time, but driven by her great need, she directed the bulbous head into the ready wetness of her cuntal opening. She was shocked. Her brain reeled with the realization of what she was doing, but there was no turning back...

He shoved... hard, and his great cock's head was forced into the tight elastic orifice, stretching it, cruelly. It felt so huge... almost as though it would tear her asunder. She was stretching, painfully, with the almost unbearable pressure he exerted. It was more than she could stand.

"Oh, God! It's too big! You'll tear me in two! Please stop!" she screamed. Her eyes brimmed with tears, as she pleaded for mercy.

Artie grimaced, as he shoved into her, harder, and she saw in his eyes that there would be no mercy. Inch by painful inch his big cock bored into her cuntal sheath, until suddenly, he rammed with all of his strength, sending his granite-hard shaft plundering far up into her tightly resisting passage with the force of a rutting bull.

Again, she screamed, *"Aieeeehhh!"* as his more than adequate, lust-inflamed prick raced full length up into the tender, coral softness of her vaginal vault, shoving up ripples of warm, resilient flesh before it, until she felt the heavy balls that swung below smack heavily against the smooth, alabaster cheeks of her helpless upturned buttocks.

His bulk lay still on top of her. He was breathing hard, the air rasping through his throat; then, he grunted and expanded his cock deep inside her cuntal passage. It flexed, muscularly, pushing out against the tightness of her soft vaginal walls, as he shoved it into her cunt another fraction of an inch.

Lauren groaned aloud. He repeated the

expanding action several more times, eliciting further moans of agony and shame from deep in her throat. Soon, she was surprised to discover that her cruelly stretched passage began to adjust to the great length and breadth of the pulsing cock deep in her well-lubricated love channel. Then, as he began to grind, slowly, into her, insinuating his prick even more tightly into her naked loins, stretching the resilient walls of her cunt until her whimpers of pain became mewls of unbidden pleasure, she began to move under him, uncontrollably in counterpoint to his revolving pelvis. Oh, I-I didn't think it would all go into me! I've got all of his huge cock... inside my cunt!

Then Artie rocked above her, goring into her with short, smooth thrustings of his cock, her body reacting of its own will, as she began to give herself over, completely, to the lewd desire of her loins... the wanton feeling of surrender bringing even more excitement to her sensate love-flesh. Summer heat lightning played there in her belly, arcing and jumping from nerve to nerve in the close, moist tightness of her vagina where Artie's giant cock had begun to thrust deeper and faster into her love-starved pussy.

Overwhelmingly, Lauren felt her whole body responding to the increased tempo and length of his cock's thrusts into her searingly vibrant cunt. She writhed and undulated beneath him, as once more his lust-distorted mouth found hers. This time, it was she who thrust her tongue deep into his mouth and throat to be sucked... and she was moaning, unceasingly, as she began to grind her passion-fired loins up to him, in tempo with his plundering cock, wanting more and more of it. Her lovely face was contorted with desire, her china blue eyes glazed and unseeing, nostrils flaring and her breath coming in jerky, raspings through her throat.

It was magnificent. Lauren had never known such rapture existed... and now, as she fucked back against him, sliding her cunt up and down the thick length of his cock, she found the sensations more intense... almost unbearable. She had never known that a man's cock could possibly give so much pleasure; likewise, she hadn't known that she would, willingly, want to give sexual joy in return. That's what she wanted now! She wanted to give herself, completely, to Artie Berman... let him do with her what he wanted. *Oh, I want it to go on and on... and on... just like this... with Artie's cock... in my cunt... fucking me... to the end of my days!*

"Keep fucking me... Artie! Fuck me... hard!" she moaned.

Now! God damn it! She's ready! He reached down, between them to the orbs of her gyrating buttocks, his hand searching for the defenseless, puckered orifice of her anus. Dipping a finger into the viscous droplets that ran in tiny rivulets from the well-stuffed cuntal passage above, he searched out the rubbery rear entrance, his finger circling it, before he placed the tip of it against the crinkled flesh. He felt the shock of her quickly indrawn breath in her body.

"Now, you'll climb the walls, baby!" he promised. "I'm going to shove my finger right up your asshole!"

God! This was it! His obscene suggestion was a further excitant to her already inflamed passion. She wanted it... insanely... wantonly... Yes! almost recklessly! She wanted it to hurt... until she screamed.

"Yes! Oh, yesssssss! Do it! Shove your finger all the way up my bottom-hole! Make me scream!" she strangled, delirious with rapture... and not knowing why she wanted it.

He shoved his finger into her hard! It surged into her backside... all the way to the palm of his hand. She screamed with the pleasure-pain of it, as his finger rotated around inside the elastic sponginess of her warm, soft, and until this moment, virginal, rectum. Never before had she felt the bittersweet combination of almost unbearable discomfort and unbelievable, sweet rapture at one and the same time.

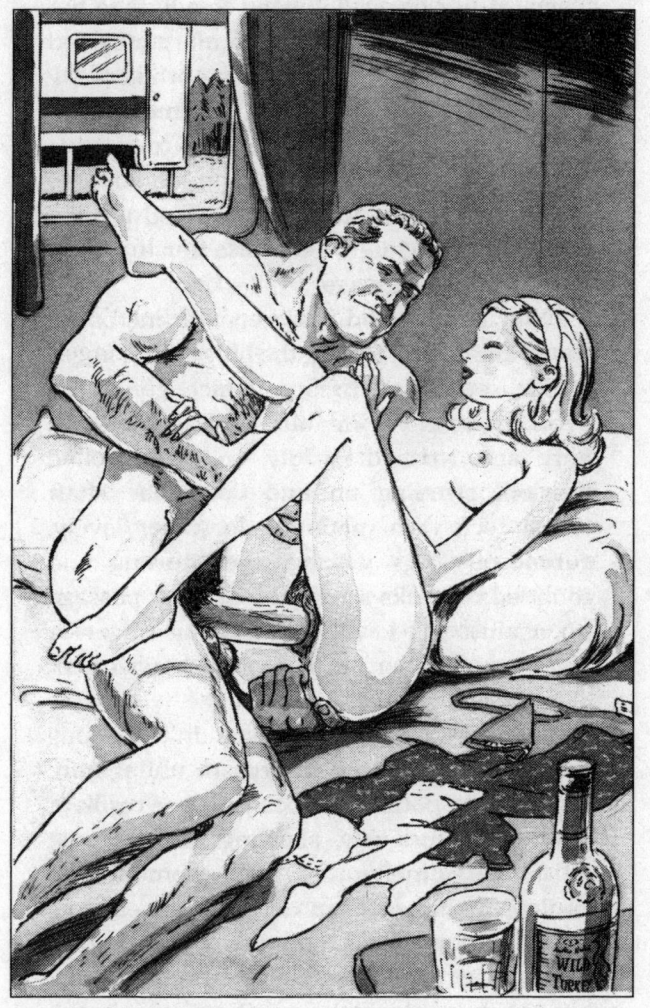

Then, as her backside began to adjust to the unnatural presence, the discomfort subsided and there was only the ecstasy of the double ravishment left to her. Now, she moved her hips back against it, attempting to skewer herself further on his torturing middle finger, while at the same time she strained to take all of his titanic cock deep into her tirelessly slaving cuntal passage.

Now, he pistoned into her with increased speed and depth, feeling the bulge of his finger in the separating tissues, which generated even more lust in him, while beneath him, she writhed, wildly, in uncontrolled passion, grinding up and down the shaft of his cock with mounting fury, her lovely, curvaceous legs jerking, toes curling and rounded buttocks screwing her back passage up against his lewdly plundering finger in abject subjugation to his double ravishment of her loins.

Then, as he knew it wouldn't be long before she convulsed in orgasm under him, he began to pound his cock into her resilient cunt flesh, furiously, showing no mercy at all for her. Finally, after long moments, he yanked his finger from her rectum, eliciting a hissing pop there; then, using both hands, he pressed her knees back, cruelly, against her chest, mashing the swelling mounds flat to her chest, where he could see the flush of her passion, the lightly tinged flesh glistening with the sweat of her rapture. Now, her whole genital plane was exposed, nakedly, defenseless to his merciless, goring attack.

Her lovely face was contorted with the sweet agony of her passion. She felt it coming. It would be soon... very soon, and she began to chant up into Artie's face.

"Oh! Ooohh! God! Oooohh! Fuck me, Artie... fuck me hard! Harder!"

Artie slaved away over Dave's wife, thrusting and plunging into her with feral energy, his pile-driving strokes becoming ever more and more forceful as he drove his big cock deeper, harder and faster into the hot, wildly clasping depths of her cuntal sheath. Damn! The only other woman I've known... who could take all of my cock... like this... is Zoe!

And then, it was there for Lauren Christie! She was in orgasm! Her head tossed, wildly, her body convulsing in wave after surging wave of muscular relaxation that ended her long agonizing wait. She spiraled to the very pinnacle, where she looked out on a beautiful dark skyscape populated by brilliant, multi-colored stars... and she was one with them, soaring free in a feeling of profound peace and well-being; then as the moment passed, she was back on the bunk in the Bermans' trailer. She was under Artie, still, his cock pounding into her like a runaway jackhammer.

The sound of her own voice was loud and unreal. She was still screaming. *"Oh my God! I'm... I'm cumming! Ahhhhhhhhhhhh!"*

Artie, pounding into her, felt the great, convulsive tremors coursing in shock waves through her body, and he knew that she was in climax, even as his own ejaculation began, deep in his belly, the burning demand searing him and inspiring him to a final, body-consuming effort.

Suddenly, explosively, his thick white sperm spewed from the slitted orifice of his cock's head to jet far up into the moist softness of her wildly clasping cunt.

"Ohhh, Lauren, baby! This's it! God*damn*... what a gorgeous cunt!" he gasped, groaningly, and fell, weakly, on top of her, all of his bulky weight resting on her torso, still cradled between her white, tapering thighs, wide-flung with obscene carelessness. He breathed heavily and harshly, the air rasping in his lungs from his great effort. His penis buried deep in her gently clasping vagina was still jerking and throbbing, as the last of his load of semen was ejaculated into a cuntal sheath that still tingled with pleasure for her.

After long minutes, as they lay exhausted, and Artie's prick was returning to its detumescent state, still lodged in her sex canal, Lauren stirred under him and said, "Well... Artie... you got... what you wanted from me... so you can let me up... now..."

"Wh-What?" he asked, drowsily.

"Get off of me! We're all finished!" she told him. "And... I-I've got to get back to the camper... and get myself straightened up... before Dave gets back!"

Artie rolled to his side, his flaccid cock pulling from her cunt with a slight pop, a long thin strand of his semen hanging, stubbornly, to the head of it.

"Hell!" he murmured, relaxing down into the soft mattress. "The real fun begins when Zoe and your husband get back here! And you're sticking around... until they do!"

Lauren flushed. "Oh, God... I-I couldn't face them... now!"

"It's all evened up!" he grunted. "They have to come in here... and face us... but with Zoe... there won't be any problem... It's Dave who'll kick up a fuss, maybe..."

"Oh, God... I-I wouldn't know what to say to him!" She was worried; perhaps unnecessarily.

CHAPTER SEVEN

Fully clothed, again, sexually satiated, feeling the closeness of the intimately shared experience, Dave and Zoe walked out of the stream bed, up the bank and regained the road.

Dave stared in disbelief. "I'll be damned! It looks like somebody's stolen your car!"

He even was more surprised to hear her carefree laughter. He looked at her questioningly.

"And, you're not worried?!"

"Not yet!" she smiled. "I think that it's just Artie's cute way of letting us know that he knows about us!"

"I hope to hell you're right because I don't remember locking it up when we left it here! It'd be a perfect setup for a car thief and I feel kind of responsible," he explained.

"Let's start worrying about it after we get back to my trailer, okay?" She looked up at the sky. "It'll be dark pretty soon, so we'd better start walking!"

"I'm sure glad it's only about a half-mile!" he grinned. "I don't think I could make it if it were any farther!"

"Why, Dave, darling... you look pretty strong to me!"

"Well... I'm a little rusty, I guess!" he kidded. "I haven't had much fucking, lately, and you just worked my tail off!"

"Poor dear!" she commiserated. "All you

need is a drink, and a little rest, before the fun thing of the evening really begins!"

"I...I'm afraid I don't follow you..."

"If my guess is right... that Artie's the one who took the car, then he saw us and knows what we were doing!" Zoe explained. "So... that means, he went after your wife... and if I know Artie, he's screwed her already. I wouldn't be surprised if we found them going at it when we get back!"

"Christ! Do you really think that?"

"Yes I do... and there'll be nothing we can do except go in... and talk it over!"

"Talk about what?"

"About us... them... all of us... together..."

"You're way ahead of me, again!" He was exasperated.

"It could develop into a nice, swinging party – with all four of us!" she laughed.

"You're kidding! Lauren'd never go for that!"

"Let's wait and see! Artie could have changed her mind – about a lot of things!"

"God, I don't know! I just don't know! It's kind of far-out..."

"It's going to be fun!" she assured him. "More fun than you've ever had before, believe me!"

***

After she had begged, tearfully, Artie had,

finally, allowed Lauren to get dressed, and he, himself, pulled on his pants and shirt. He was mixing fresh drinks, when Zoe came through the door of the trailer, followed by a sheepish looking Dave Christie, who was more than a little uncertain about the whole thing. He didn't dare look at his wife, who sat, demurely, at the breakfast nook, and she, in turn, kept her gaze averted. The fact that she was there said it all, for both of them...

It was the Bermans who carried it off. Zoe bustled over to Artie, patted him on the cheek and gave him a kiss, remarking, at the same time, "Artie... I brought Dave back with me! He was very good to me..."

Artie handed Dave Christie a highball, then carried the other one to Lauren. Handing it to her, he said, "You've got a rare gem of a woman here, Dave! And, Zoe and I'd like to get to know both of you... even better than we do, now."

Going back to the built-in bar, he fixed two more bourbons. Dave didn't know what to say. He took a large swallow of his drink and sat down opposite Lauren.

Berman was going on, "Shall we drink to it?" He hoisted his glass up; Zoe, drink in hand, beside him smiled encouragingly at Dave.

Dave was perplexed. "If I understand this right, Zoe was suggesting that we join you in a..." He stopped, not quite able to articulate it, correctly.

"In a swinging party?" Artie queried, looking at his wife, Zoe.

"Yeah... swapping... or group sex... I guess you call it?" Dave said, "In the long run, I guess it's sort of up to Lauren..." He reached across the table and lifted her chin, forcing her to look him square in the face. "How about it, darling?"

He saw the scratches on her face and arms and knew that it was she who had crashed through the underbrush, on the bank, above them, while he had been driving his cock deep into Zoe's soft belly. His wife had seen them! She knew... just as he knew... or could guess accurately about what had happened in the Bermans' trailer, a few minutes ago.

Lauren' deep blue eyes were glistening with tears, as she looked into her husband's face. "Oh, Dave!" she sobbed. "I didn't intend f-for anything to h-happen... but it went on and on, a-and pretty soon... I-I couldn't help it! It j-just happened!"

"Do you... want to do it?"

"You mean... stay here... and do it... some more... all four of us?"

"Yes... that's what Artie means!"

It was such a strange turn of events... so confusing to her and yet her fevered coupling with Artie had been so, all-consuming, so satisfactory. Now, she realized that even their talk about it was working on her. She was becoming aroused, all over, again... just thinking about the possibilities...

"Y-yes Dave..." she said, her voice soft and faltering. "I'd like t-to do it!"

He leaned across the table and kissed his wife, soundly, on the lips; then picking up his drink, he said, "Okay, Artie... we'll drink to that!"

It was the beginning of an extrordinary and thrilling evening for all four of them...

***

It was pitch dark. Dipstick MacKay made his way over to Hunter Mitchell's sleeping bag. He could tell, instantly, that Billie occupied it with him. She was stretched out on top of the gang leader... and Dipstick didn't have to exercise much imagination as to the activity going on inside.

"Hunter!" he hissed. "It's me... Dipstick!"

"Yeah... what do you want?"

"I thought you'd like to know... about some of the things I saw, tonight..." Dipstick offered.

"Like what?"

"Well... like the guy from the camper's been banging that black-haired broad you were hot for..." He stopped, waiting for

Hunter's comment.

"That right?" Hunter said, rolling Billie from on top of him and leaning up on an elbow. "Tell me more!"

"And the big guy, the black-haired broad's husband was banging the other guy's wife... now they're all over in the trailer together... and they're starting a party with all four! They're all bare-assed naked... already!"

"Is that other broad the blonde one... that was wearing the hot pants?" Hunter asked.

"Yeah... it is!"

The black-bearded leader smiled in the darkness. Damn! That's perfect! Both of them together... that cute blonde... and Zoe! His mind was working, making plans... considering the things he would like to do... would do... especially to Zoe Berman. He owed her some special treatment!

"You know, Dipstick he said, grudgingly, "I hate to say this, but sometimes you come up with some pretty good ideas! Get the other guys and we'll have a council! Maybe we'll have ourselves some fun tonight!"

Billie Grant snuggled up close to him again. They were both naked. "Hunter..." she murmured, "I'm all hot for you already! Will you fuck me... first? Please?"

"Not tonight, baby! I'm going to save it for those two broads in the trailer!" he growled. "Besides, don't forget, like I told you, before, there're two guys there, too! You can have some fun with them... if you've really got to be fucked!"

There was one thing bothering her. "Sure, Hunter I understand... but you're not going to... to hurt those people are you?"

"Goddamn it... I told you not to interfere with me!" he growled. "I ought give you a few smacks – but I haven't got time!" He crawled out of the sleeping bag to stand naked in the night over her. "So get your ass out of there and get some clothes on!"

"I don't want to go," she whimpered, "if anyone's going to get hurt!"

"You're going!" he said with finality... "And, nobody'll get hurt if they cooperate. But I can't guarantee anything if somebody tries to do something dumb!"

Reaching down, Hunter drew on his pants, as he saw the other three men approaching. Yes! Tonight's the night... for fun and games!

Even though Lauren had said that she would join in a group sex party, there was a certain disparity between the saying and the doing; however, under the expert guidance of Artie and Zoe Berman, she was coaxed out of her clothing, again. All four lay on the double bunk bed, finishing up the last of another of Artie's potent drinks, and as the alcohol began to take its effect, she began to respond, sexually to Dave, on the one side, Artie on the other, while below, Zoe ran her hands, tantalizingly, over her body, her fingers, feather-light, as she stimulated the soft, white flesh of her inner thighs and moved upward to the gently pulsing furrow, where glowing hot coals of her desire were being fanned into flame once more. Dave was kissing her, deeply, his tongue searching the honeyed sweetness of her mouth; at the same time, Artie licked and sucked at a pink, tumescent nipple, his big hands cupping the full mound of a breast up to his avid mouth.

She felt her arousal building, sensations of such magnitude coursing through her, that she knew it would be only a matter of a few minutes until... she would be caught, helplessly, in the grip of her passion. Never before had she begun to respond so soon... but then three people were concentrating their attentions on her. God... oh, God... so many hands... and so many mouths! They'll drive me wild! It felt so good to her, and she wanted it... wanted them... especially, she wanted her husband, Dave! It was so nice to have him there... being a part of it. It gave her an extra, guilt-free, feeling of confidence and security.

***

Outside, moving swiftly, silently, in the darkness, five figures ranged alongside the Bermans' trailer, waiting while the leader stood at one of the curtained windows and surveyed the erotic tableau of the two couples on the big, built-in bunk bed.

Looks like they're just getting started! The big guy... with the hair must be Berman... Zoe's husband! He's the one we'll have to be careful with... he could be dangerous!

He tried the door. It was open. Good! Less chance of a slip-up! Hunter opened the door and walked, boldly, into the trailer. He was followed closely by Gavin Rust and Frank Superini. Dipstick MacKay remained outside, for the time being, as a lookout. Billie Grant was with him.

Zoe saw them first. As she saw movement in her peripheral vision, she turned her head to glance toward the door. She gasped, "My God... it's Hunter!" Opening her mouth to scream, she suddenly found herself muzzled by his restraining hand, as Hunter reached her in two strides. She heard his voice from behind his black-bearded lips hiss at her, "Don't make one sound... if you don't want to get hurt."

She watched with horrified eyes, as the second man, smaller, ferret-like, clapped a hand over Lauren' mouth as she struggled to sit up, from between the two men. She had heard Zoe's gasp... the swift movement of feet and realized that something was wrong.

"Son-of-a-bitch!" Artie Berman gritted, coming up with both fists balled, ready to fight. He subsided, instantly; he was looking into the barrel of a .38 caliber pistol, held in the rock-steady hand of Hunter Mitchell.

Dave, likewise, had sensed the danger. He had begun to gather his body for a lunge at the smaller man, nearest him, who was holding his hand over Lauren' mouth. "What the hell!" he shouted. The third man, leaned forward, his gun pointing at Dave's head. "Shut up!" he warned. Dave saw a good-looking youth with pale, blue eyes and almost white hair. It was Frank Superini. There was an absolute silence for a beat; then Artie Berman demanded, "What do you bums want?"

"We've just invited ourselves to your little party!" Hunter Mitchell told them, an evil grin parting his bearded lips.

"Like hell!"

The gang leader looked at him, hard, his face set and grim. "We're here already, and we've got the muscle and the hardware to make it go our way; but nobody'll get hurt if you just play it cool. Don't do anything stupid... foolish... or heroic... understand?"

"You'll never get away with it!" Dave ground out at them!

"We'll see!" Hunter answered curtly. "Tie the guys up!"

Only then did he take his hand away from Zoe's mouth. She looked up at him through eyes miserable with fright.

"Hunter!" she whispered. "If it's me... you want... just take me! These other people... don't have anything to do with it!"

Gavin Rust released Lauren and, while Frank Superini stood guard, went to the door and said, "Right *on!* Hunter wants the guys tied up!"

Meanwhile, Hunter glared down at Zoe, his eyes mean, full of anger. "Baby, there's no more talk – just action now!" He stepped back and gave the two naked men his orders: "Move down to the other bed... at the front there!"

Dave and Artie clambered off the bed and moved, warily, to the front of the trailer, where Dipstick and Billie waited for them with rolls of wide surgical tape in their hands. They had no choice to do otherwise. They were both bareassed naked and faced with four armed men, who probably wouldn't hesitate to use the weapons they held in their hands. The odds weren't so great.

"On the bed!" MacKay ordered.

The two husbands lay down on the bed. Quickly and efficiently, Dipstick and Billie bound them, using the surgical tape. In a few moments, Dave and Artie lay, trussed, hand and foot, and for extra measure... tape was placed over their mouths, as well.

Hunter inspected the two immobilized

men. "Good!" he spat and turned his attention to the two women huddled together on the bed. Lauren was sobbing with fright, as she clung to Zoe, asking in a hoarse whisper, "A-Are they... going t-to d-do... what I-I think?"

"God! I-I don't know! But... I'll try to get Hunter t-to leave you alone!"

Gavin Rust leered at them. "Damn! Hunter can sure pick them!" he reached out to one of Zoe's superb full breasts, his fingers digging cruelly into her smooth, soft flesh. "Christ! I can't wait to get my mouth on these!" he grunted.

"Drop it, Gavin!" the bearded leader ordered. "The blonde's the one that gets it!"

The smaller man drew his hand back, as though he had touched a hot stove. He grinned, sheepishly, and turned his salacious, ferret-like eyes on Lauren. "There's not much difference... I guess..." His hand caressed Lauren' breasts, cupping one in his hand, his moistly warm lips encompassed a pink nipple, sucking up the aureole as well.

Lauren shrank back and cried, "D-Don't! Oh, p-please don't!"

Zoe's grey eyes met Hunter's, defiantly, "Tell your goon to leave Lauren alone! It's me you want isn't it?"

"Yeah but I'm saving you until last!" he grunted. "You're going to watch... while I show you what you missed! Then if I feel like it I might fuck you, too!"

Slowly, deliberately, he began to pull off his clothing. This was apparently a signal to the other three men, for they, too, began undressing.

Whispering urgently into Zoe's ear, Lauren asked, "My God! you *know* him?"

"Yes... in a way," Zoe whispered back.

"What's this a-all about?"

"It's a long story. I'll have to tell you about it... later."

Hunter heard. He came to sit on the bed. Lauren crawled away from him, into a far corner of the bunk. Watching her, amusedly, he said, "It's not such a long story! This bitch's a little pricktease... and she picked the wrong guy! That's all!" Lauren could only stare at his terrifying nakedness, his long, tumescent cock lengthening obscenely in little incremental jerks between his thighs...

Then, he stretched out on the bed, reached over and pulled Lauren over to him. "So... your name's Lauren? You're the one who was wearing those sexy hot pants! Come here! I'm going to fuck you!" he grunted. "But before I do... we're going to have some fun!" He encircled her body with a strong arm. "Meanwhile... Zoe, you little bitch... see if you can get my cock real hard with your mouth... and be goddamned sure you do it right!"

Now Gavin was naked. His body was scrawny, but a bountiful nature had supplied him with a cock that was every bit a match for Artie Berman's. He climbed onto the bed and stretched out on the other side of Lauren Christie, plastering his body up against hers. His pole-like erection was digging into the smooth flesh of her buttocks. She cringed with the contact, her eyes brimming with tears. Oh, God... not two of them... Of course, earlier, Artie had told her that part of the fun of swinging was multiple copulation. She had considered it... had even consented to it, with her husband, Dave... and Artie... but with these men complete strangers? Dear God!!

Mitchell pulled her head over to his, his avid mouth finding her lips to kiss her. His full, black beard tickled her face. She tried to turn her head aside, but he held her hard and steady. "God damn it!" he hissed. "I'd hate to mark up your pretty face!" He captured her lips and snaked his tongue deep into her mouth to savour her moist, sweet mouth.

Meanwhile, Zoe knelt over Hunter's loins. She saw that his big cock was only partially erect. Without hesitation, she leaned over him and took the half-hardened shaft of his penis in her hand to skin back the heavy foreskin, her other hand going under him, to cup his heavy scrotal sac and play with his balls. She was worried. It was not about herself. She was experienced enough to handle whatever came her way... But Lauren... she's as innocent as a sacrificial lamb! Damn! I hope she doesn't get hurt!

Lowering her head, then, she took the head of Hunter's cock into her mouth, her tongue laving all around the growing corona, her lips tucked in over her teeth; she exerted pressure all the way around as her cheeks began to hollow in a sucking motion. She felt his prick pulsing to full erection in her mouth, and she began to bob her head, slowly, her lips slipping down further and further over him, until she was absorbing almost all of him into her mouth and his glans was hitting against the back of her throat.

Hunter shoved his hips up at her mouth, countering the slow rhythm she had set. He intuitively knew she would know how to do it properly. Her mouth was smooth, moist warm... and practiced.

Frank Superini watched Zoe for a moment, his cock throbbing to erection. He climbed onto the bed with the others, reminding himself that in a few moments he'd make her do the same thing to him. Christ! It makes me hot just watching her, the way she's going after Hunter's big cock, but meanwhile... His eyes zeroed in on Lauren' frizz of golden pubic hair at the base of her sweet little belly, seeing the curving swell of her hips, her sleek thighs framing the center of his interest. Training his eyes up farther, he saw that Gavin had one of her stiff, perky nipples in his mouth, sucking noisily on it, while his other hand cupped up the other breast, the alabaster smoothness showing the marks of his cruel fingers. Hunter was kissing her, deeply, his mouth welded to hers, as he held her in his tight grip.

Lauren, lying between the two men, being kissed by the bearded one called Hunter, suddenly remembered: Oh, God! He's the one I-I listened to... and watched... while he was... was fucking that young girl, Billie... on the sleeping bag! Vividly, she recalled her thoughts... her feelings; she had wanted to be that girl... wanted to lie under him... and take his cock deep into her seething cunt! Now... here he was... And he's going t-to... rape m-me!

She didn't want it! A person would think that in the face of her fear and terror, she would have been numbed... refusing to believe that it could happen... that his rape of her was a reality that would take place in a very few minutes; yet how was it... that there was a certain, sex-laden thrill keening through her body, the warm glow there in her belly, the definite sensation of wetness forming down there, between her legs... all indicating sexual arousal... in a woman who was about to be sexually assaulted... raped, fucked against her will?

Then Lauren felt another pair of hands. They caressed her hips and thighs, gently massaging them, then played over the triangle of her loins, unseen fingers playing with the golden curls a moment or two before one slid into the exposed crease at the top of her cuntal slit, to find the sensitive shaft of her re-awakening clitoris. She was being held so tightly between Hunter and Gavin that she couldn't see who it was that was teasing her genitals.

Now, those hands lifted her knees up, flexing them, then her thighs were pried apart, firmly and she knew that the whole of her loins was exposed, nakedly, to that unseen, unknown man. God! Which one of them is it? Desperately, she tried to close her legs, again, but his greater strength held them apart. Her muscles trembled, painfully, as she played a serious tug-of-war with him. Finally, she could resist no longer. Her muscles relaxed and her thighs splayed open, her fluttering cunt widely... utterly revealed. She heard the man's sadistic chuckle of triumph. She fully expected to feel his body coming between her thighs, his stiff penis entering her unwanting vagina to plunge into her without mercy... fucking her in mindless fury.

It didn't happen like that; instead, she felt those hands move upward on the fearful soft flesh of her inner thighs, until they were on either side of her golden-haired outer labia... Then, very plainly, she felt his thumbs slowly, tantalizingly, spread them apart to reveal thecoral inner lips, already glistening with her exudate.

At the other end of the trailer, securely trussed up and lying helplessly on the other bunk bed, Dave could only watch, with mounting fury, as the three men mauled and stimulated his wife. He could hear and see, but he was effectively gagged by the wide tape across his mouth. *Fucking bastards! They'd better not hurt her! But, even if I got free, what could I do?* There were four men... all armed, not counting the smooth-faced boy, with the light, blue eyes who seemed not to have a gun. Desperately, his eyes searched the trailer for something... anything... that might be a help to him, either to escape, or as a weapon. There was nothing. His eyes came back to the other bed. The big, bearded man was kissing Lauren, while the smaller one licked and sucked at her breasts. Below, the good-looking man seemed to be getting ready to mount her. He was spreading her thighs apart, and his long, thin cock stood out from his loins, throbbingly. Then as he watched, Frank Superini lowered his head between her trembling thighs, and Dave suddenly knew what he was going to do.

Shit! He's going to go down on her! Lick

and suck her pussy! Christ, even I've never done that to her! She's never let me try, but tonight – before these goons broke in on us – I think she would have gone for it!

The fourth man, he noticed, had stayed near the door, but now, he, too, began to strip his clothing off. The young boy was still fully clothed. When Dipstick MacKay was finally standing there, naked, he looked toward the tableau on the bed and saw that there was no place for him, there, yet, remembering Hunter's admonition that the black-haired bitch, who was kneeling over the leader's loins with his big cock in her mouth, was not to be touched by any of the gang, he turned to Billie and said, "Get it up for me… Billie!" He reached down to grasp and lift his slowly hardening cock by the shaft, as without hesitation, the small, pixie-like boy knelt before him and took his prick into his mouth.

It was only a foot from Dave's face. He watched with revulsion, as his small hands reached under to titillate the big man's balls, his mouth beginning to absorb more and more of the rapidly growing cock. *Damn fag! Pretty boy! Christ! It's disgusting!*

After a few moments, Dipstick began to move his hips backward and forward, to drive more of his fully erect cock deep into the boy's mouth and throat; then, suddenly, he withdrew it and growled, "That's enough!

Now... why don't you have your fun with these guys... while I'm busy with that blonde bitch!"

Dave was appalled. Tied up as he and Artie were... they would be helpless! This young faggot could do anything with them he wanted! For the first time since the motorcycle gang had invaded the trailer, he felt a slamming fear in his guts. There's no telling what the little fag'll do! He considered the possibilities: *He could force us to suck him off... fuck him in the ass... or... he might want to shove his prick up our assholes! Christ!* It was a grim picture he conjured... and he didn't like it at all!

He watched as Dipstick walked to the other end of the trailer and crawled up on the bed. There was a general shifting of people, then... but he wasn't able to watch it all.

His attention was drawn, fully, to the small, leather-clad figure, who sat down on the bed next to him... and whose small hand reached out to his now flaccid prick, "Hunter said... if I wanted to... I could make it with you two..." The voice was high, musical... almost like a woman's voice, but Dave tried to roll his hips away, strangled noises coming from his mouth through the gag.

"Oh... you can't talk!" He reached up to remove the tape from his mouth.

"Now... what do you want to say?"

Highway to Shame

"Keep your hands off of me you damned faggot!" Dave grunted.

A trilling laugh tinkled from those too-pretty lips. "That's funny... almost too funny for words! It's true they call me Billie, but..."

Then, Dave watched in amazement, as Billie removed her jacket and tossed it aside. Next her boy's shirt was slowly unbuttoned to reveal a pair of the loveliest woman's breasts he had ever seen. They were small, firm, pouting upward, and the nipples, small, berry-like were hardening into little nubs of sensitive flesh. Whipping off the shirt, she was nude from the waist up.

"Does that look like I could be a gay one?" she asked, challengingly.

Dave stared at the beauty before him and gasped, "God... I wouldn't have believed it! You're beautiful"

"And, all the rest of me matches!" she told him with a smile. "Now do you want me to touch you... or not?"

Below, unbidden, his big cock was throbbing to erection. "It sure as hell puts things in a different light... but it's going to be hard for me... to do anything for you... tied up like this..." he suggested.

"I-I couldn't let you go!" she explained. "Hunter would kill me!"

Then, she reached over to remove the tape from Artie's mouth. As soon as he was stripped of the gag, he said, "Baby... if you let us go... I can guarantee you the best fuck you've ever had!"

"I-I can't do it... so don't ask me, again!"

Billie removed her jeans, boots, socks and panties. She was completely nude, as she crawled up on the bed with Dave and Artie. She went on, "But, don't worry... we'll all have a good time!" Her eyes swept down to gaze at the two big cocks spearing up, fully hardened... and ready. The young 'boy' gave a throaty chuckle. "I know I'll be satisfied... you've both got cocks that don't stop!"

With studied casualness, she knee walked over and straddled Dave's face, then leaning forward and to the side, she grasped Artie's outsize cock, her little hand not able to encircle its girth; at the same time, she lowered her loins down over Dave's face. "First... we'll do a little cock-sucking... and cunt-licking!" she instructed.

Dave looked up into the tender, moist furrow above him, and just as soon as she dropped her loins down into range, his tongue shot out to bury itself in the liquid depths of her pulsing, needy young cunt. An unbidden moan of desire escaped his lips, as he savoured the sweet tang of her dripping pink folds of her vaginal mouth. Yes! Things had certainly changed in just a few moments. His only wish was that his hands could be free; it would really be fun, then...

As Billie's lips came down over his cock's head, throbbing lustily with desire, Artie muttered, "Suck it... good, Billie, baby! Suck it good!" His hips thrust up at her... and she began to bob her head expertly over him. Damn! This's something! Imagine! Me, big Artie Berman... being raped by a little slip of a girl!

In another part of the trailer, Lauren lay between two virile men, a third down below, using his hands to pull apart the cringing petals of her moistly throbbing cunt. She was terror-stricken, as she felt the wash of warm air over her exposed flesh. Oh, he's going t-to... use his mouth on m-me!

She felt her cheeks flame at the thought. She had never allowed Dave to do it to her... but now... she could do nothing to stop it! It was going to happen... and she didn't even know who it was!

Suddenly, then, the moist warmth of his tongue was there. She felt it wiggle right into her vaginal orifice. His tongue was actually inside her, now! Oh, God, no! She tried to screw her hips down into the mattress to escape that vile act... but it was no use. His long, agile oral member plunged in and out of her, then moved in tantalizing circles just inside her cuntal opening. The glowing warmth of her arousal was suddenly fanned into roaring flames, as intense sexual sensations keened, excitingly, in her belly.

She moaned, helplessly, up into Hunter's avid mouth... and she suddenly, realized that she wasn't trying to back away from that hot, probing tongue in her cunt. She was undulating her hips up to meet the mouth that tantalized so tormentingly, there below, in her exquisitely raw love flesh.

Hunter raised his head, breaking the long kiss, and growled at Zoe, "That's enough sucking, bitch!"

She was disappointed. She was hoping that she would be able to suck him to ejaculation, her reasoning being that it would save Lauren from his punishing cock; although, the time had seemed to pass so slowly, it had been but a very few minutes since the motorcycle gang had stormed into the trailer. She didn't stop immediately. Doggedly, she went on bobbing her head over him.

Reaching down, the bearded leader grabbed a handful of her shiny black hair and hauled her head up off his pulsingly ready prick; then his other hand swung in a short arc, his open palm catching her full in the face. The crack of his hand on the soft flesh of her face was loud in the trailer. "When I tell you something, you do it, right then!" he seethed through clenched, angry teeth.

It hurt! God! It hurt, terribly, but Zoe would not cry. He wouldn't make her cry! She raised up and leaned back on her heels.

Glaring at him, defiantly, she hissed, "Okay, big man, you're the boss! Do you get your kicks by beating up on women?"

"And, what if I do?"

"You're sick!"

CRACK! Hunter's hand slashed at her face, again.

"Sick!" Zoe howled.

CRACK!

"Siiiiickkkkk!" she screamed, collapsing back on the bed, her eyes streaming from the pain of his punishing slaps.

"I'll take care of you later!" he growled, motioning Frank Superini away from his kneeling position between Lauren' fear-trembling legs.

Lauren had watched in wide-eyed fear and horror as the tough, black-bearded leader had delivered those hurtful blows to Zoe's beautiful face. Oh, God h-he's some kind of a sadistic lunatic!

Frank Superini was stretched out beside her, now, and his hands began to roam down across the curve of her belly and smooth back up to her breast, removing Gavin's hand from it; then, he too dropped his head down to take the hardened coral nipple into his mouth. He used his teeth to nibble on it, painfully... but even so, she loved the tingling sensuality of it despite herself, her breast seeming to swell and push up at his mouth. There was a hungry mouth on each breast now, and she looked up pleadingly at Hunter Mitchell as he leered down into her face and told her, "Baby... you're going to get fucked... like you've never been fucked before!"

"P-Please... don't?" she begged. "I-I've... never..."

"Never... what?"

"Done it with more than one... m-man!" she trembled.

"Then... it'll be even more fun because you're going to be stuffed with cock every place it's possible to put one!"

"Oh... Gooodddddd! Noooooooooo!" she wailed, her imagination working overtime, the bizarre, vile ideas slashing through her brain... leaving her almost in shock. H-He can't mean that... it's monstrous... inhuman!

Gavin Rust looked up from her breast he was mauling and asked, "Hunter when do we start on the real fun things?"

"Hell... anytime you want except that I'm going to fuck her in the cunt!" the gang leader grunted, as he dropped his head down between her thighs, his tongue lashing out to the short, hardened length of her twitching clitoris.

Ecstatic sensations throbbed there, as he licked her several times before taking the sensitive bud between his teeth, lightly, his hotly moist tongue dancing directly on the nerve-rich head of the miniature phallus. She couldn't hold back her moan of surprised pleasure; it just came tumbling out of her mouth.

Dipstick MacKay crawled onto the bed just then, looking for a piece of the action. Gavin Rust chose that moment to kneel up; growlingly, he told Bill on the other side of her, "Move your ass, Superboy... I'm going to try something!"

Grumbling, Bill moved away, enough to allow the small, bandy-legged Rust to straddle Lauren' chest. She looked up at him through her tears, her eyes pleading, but he ignored her tears, telling her, "Listen, baby... I'm going to fuck you between the tits... so you hold them up with your hands... and kind of push them together... understand?"

Lauren tilted her head down to look between her quivering breasts. She saw Gavin's short but very thick cock jutting out, menacingly, and as she gasped with disbelief of the thing he wanted to do, he spat into the palm of his hand, reached down and gripped the fat shaft of his cock and, slowly, stroked the foreskin back to reveal it's shiny, throbbing head. With deliberate slowness, he rubbed his saliva all over it.

"Damn if you haven't got the prettiest pair of snubbers I've ever seen!" he chortled, his ferret eyes looking over her breasts with salacious desire.

She had made no move to follow his instructions. "Get them pushed up... like I told you!"

"N-No!" she told him. "That's horrible..."

"You got no choice... Baby-Doll! Frank... do it for her... and make damn sure you hold them tight!"

Frank Superini knelt at her head, and reaching out to the soft, swelling mounds of her tingling breasts, pushed them up, cupping them from the sides, until the valley between them was closed; then Gavin Rust flexed his hips forward to drive his heavy cock between them. She felt it bulk against the cringing softness of her satiny smooth flesh, as it forced its way into the confined space. Oh, God... I n-never thought of this!

Leaning forward, now, Gavin began to plunge in and out of the narrow valley between her breasts. She felt the moistly warm shaft, throbbing against the sensitive flesh... while below Hunter's tongue was driving her wild with desire, as it stabbed in and out of her now searingly ecstatic cuntal passage, and when his tongue worked down, momentarily, to play, moistly, warmly, on the puckered flesh of her anus, she moaned with the abject humiliation of it. Yet at the same time her hips bucked up to that tormenting tongue for more of the same.

MacKay had watched as Gavin crawled

up to straddle of the blonde to begin fucking her between the tits. He decided to wait; there was nothing he could do right then, but there was the black-haired bitch. She was still curled up, sobbing from the hurts Hunter had inflicted. Billie, in the other end of the trailer was naked, now, and she was crawling up into the bunk where Dave and Artie lay tied hand and foot. So that left Zoe. With strong hands he pulled her up.

"Get up on your knees!" he ordered.

Zoe obeyed him, silently, getting up on all fours, her full found naked buttocks waving, whitely, in the air. Dipstick MacKay moved in behind her. He was interested only in straight fucking, right then. His cock lanced out, rigid and ready, and without further preparation, he grasped his rock-hard cock, directed it to the pulsing opening of her cunt and rammed it into her, hard. It was a dry entrance, but he didn't care, as with animal force he plundered her, his cock going into the soft cuntal flesh like an unpeeled log.

"OOoohh!" Zoe groaned. "Wait... ahhh!... at least wait until... I'm... unhh!... ready!"

MacKay, knowing that he was defying his leader, Hunter Mitchell, merely withdrew until only the lust-inflated head of his demanding prick remained in the abraded vestibule of her vagina, then gripping her hips above the swelling curve, he gored into her, again and again, fucking her, animalistically.

After a few moments of this, Zoe began to feel the sensations of sexual need, and her hips began to waggle back at him, countering his feral, plunging cock.

Lauren, lying there, with Gavin Rust astraddle her chest, mindlessly, shoving his cock in and out, between her breasts, while Bill held them up, pushing them together, to form the channel of warm, satiny flesh into which he thrust, using the space between as a surrogate cunt, was helpless to stop it. Her mind was in a daze. She was responding, against her will, to the tongue Hunter Mitchell shot into her in time to the flexing hips of Gavin Rust. Oh... I-I can't stand it! His t-tongue's... *soooo* good... and I can't help it! She remembered how she had listened and watched as this same man had sucked... and fucked that girl called Billie that night, on the sleeping bag. God! How hot she had been! How much she had wanted it then! Now... it's about to happen... for real! Oh, God! I'm going to get it! I'm going to have a strange man's cock... i-in me... fucking me! Now!

Without thought, unconsciously, her hands drifted up to cup themselves under Frank Superini's hands. Realizing, instantly, what she wanted, he slipped his hands away, and her hands replaced his. She was cupping her tingling breasts up around the fat, pulsing cock that slid wetly between them. She looked up at Gavin Rust's face. His eyes were closed. He breathed, raspily, through his mouth, which was hanging open, almost witlessly, as he pumped back and forth, driving his cock into the soft whiteness of the tight channel between Lauren's generously proportioned breasts. Suddenly, she realized that he was almost ready to cum... and now, below, her hips ground up to Hunter's mouth, countering his rhythmic tonguing of her desire-filled cunt... wanting it to be filled with rampaging cock.

With a quick, forceful, final thrust, Gavin Rust came. His cock jerked, spewing his cum into the hollow of her breasts, as he held himself rigidly immobile, his face reflecting the animal satisfaction he felt as his lewd sperm was emptied from him. "Christ!" he gasped. "That's... almost as good as a tight cunt!"

Lauren felt the flooding, sticky warmth of his cum, as it jetted from him. A few drops landed on her upper lip and cheek. Strangely, she felt a certain tingle of increased sexual stimulation in the knowledge that she had given him a measure of satisfaction as he had fucked her in that unlikely place. But he's really... a-a rapist! They're forcing me... a-all of them!

Frank Superini growled, "Okay, Gavin crawl the hell off... Hunter and me... are going to do the job right, now!"

Reluctantly, Gavin Rust withdrew his still jerking prick from the channel of mammary flesh, and leaning to the side, he threw his leg off, over her, rolling to his side to collapse into a satiated heap. Lauren still held her breasts aloft and together, not knowing what to do for the spreading, liquid puddle of sperm. Surprisingly, it was Frank Superini, who spotted the box of tissues. He took a handful of them and handed them to Gavin. "Clean her up!" he told him, his voice brittle.

Gavin glared at him, but he did it, swabbing up his white, viscous semen from between her breasts. Slowly, she released them, allowing him to wipe her chest clean.

At that point, Hunter raised his head from her twitching, fluttering cunt. He looked balefully at thet terrified young wife and said, "You're hot, bitch! Hot enough to be fucked, now!"

His eyes swung around the interior of the trailer. Billie was getting her kicks with the two squares, tied up on the bed. Superboy was kneeling just above Lauren' head, his big cock held in his hand, caressingly, waiting none too patiently for Bill Rust to finish wiping up his spunk on her chest... and behind him, at the foot of the big double bunk, Dipstick MacKay was slamming his big cock into Zoe, from behind. She was fucking back at him, furiously...

Hunter's anger was instantaneous and terrible. "You God damned son-of-a-bitch, Dipstick... I told you to leave her for last... for me to fuck!" he roared.

"So... what are you going to do about it... now?" MacKay shot back, insolently.

"Nothing – right now – but when we're finished here, so God help me I'll kill you!" Hunter stormed.

Then, turning back to Lauren, he wedged himself down between her legs and guided his long thick cock directly into her cuntal passage. Driven by his fury, he plunged his big cudgel of a prick into her with cruel force, ramming it home in the tender flesh of her pussy with one deep, penetrating thrust.

She screamed loud, once, before Frank Superini clapped a hand over her mouth. "Shut up... bitch!" he hissed into her ear, while below, Hunter maddened with anger, slammed into her without mercy, his big cock powering in and out of her cuntal passage like a pile-driver.

Working himself around, reversing his position, while at the same time, keeping Lauren gagged, Frank flung a leg over to straddle her chest; then, he looked down at her, his lust-filled eyes gleaming points of light blue steel, as he told her, "Now... baby, you get to eat my cock! Turn your lips over your teeth, and make damned sure you don't try any funny stuff! You hurt me at all and

I'll knock your head off, understand?"

He took his hand away and guided his long thin cock to her lips. "Take it in your mouth!" he commanded.

"OOoohh, God! N-No!" she shuddered, attempting to turn her head aside.

One strong hand, the fingers entangled in her golden blonde hair, turned her head back straight; the other clamped hard on the muscles at the hinge of her jaw, forcing her mouth open and before she could voice further objection. Superboy's cock was in her mouth. "Remember what I told you!" he threatened, thrusting his angry face an inch from her own.

Helpless in his grasp, she obeyed him abjectly, shielding her teeth by turning her lips over them, then ovaling them around the shaft of his prick. God! What else can I-I do?

It was, surprisingly, silky soft, almost rubbery in her mouth, and there was a tangy flavour that seemed not at all unpleasant... but she was revulsed with the unnaturalness of it.

"Now use your tongue!" Superini urged.

Experimentally, Lauren swirled her tongue around the throbbing corona and felt the erotic shock of it in him, as his cock's head pulsed and expanded inside her mouth.

Then, with short, slow strokes, be moved it in and out of her lips, shoving in a little more of his long, slender length with each deliberate movement. As more and more of his shaft was absorbed into her mouth and throat, she gagged and coughed up some drooling saliva... but there was no escaping it; he just kept moving, steadily, paying no attention to her distress.

"You'll get used to it!" he growled, finally. "You can start doing some sucking on it... and before you're through it's going to be going right down your throat!"

God! How m-much more of it... c-can I take?

Below, Hunter had been pounding into her so hard, that she could do nothing, but now her whole body was responding to the two men. She began to move up against him, wanting to take all of him deep into her lust-incited cunt. She couldn't help it. She wanted it... wanted to be fucked hard and deep. Then, she was conscious that her throat was relaxed and she was beginning to take Frank Superini's cock as deeply into her mouth and throat as Hunter's outsize prick was storming into her needful cunt. Sexual rapture was overwhelming her, as she sucked and licked, wildly, at the huge presence in her mouth, at the same time as her hips rose to take all of the bearded gang leader's cock into her throbbing cunt.

On the bed, at the other end of the trailer, Billie, who had been licked to steaming readiness by Dave Christie while at the same time she had sucked Artie Berman's thrilling, massive cock to pulsating white heat, shifted her position. Straddling Artie's helpless body, she reached back to guide his long thick shaft to the tender, young orifice of her pussy; then dropping her weight down on him, she absorbed his titanic cock to its full length and breadth. "Oh... My God!" she gasped with surprise, as she realized the true enormity of it. "Damn! You *are* big!" Then, as she began to work her hips, forcing her cunt to ride up and down that great shaft she had absorbed, she turned passion-filled eyes to Dave and murmured, "If you hitch yourself around... so I can get at you... I'll suck you off... at the same time!"

Dave had been terribly worked up by his licking and sucking at her moistly pink cunt... but that was all he could do. Both he and Artie were at the mercy of her sexual whims... and he had been disappointed when she had crawled over to impale herself on Artie's big cock. Needless to say, he began squirming and snaking his body upward in the bed until, she could lean down to capture his hard, lancing cock in her mouth. God! She was an expert! Her tongue drove him wild as she licked and sucked his cock, frequently swooping down to lick his balls and even occasionally tongue his anus; at the same time her whole body rose and fell on

Artie's rock-hard prick.

As Dipstick MacKay gored into Zoe from behind, ramming his cock hard and deep into her, she knew that she was hanging on the edge of her orgasm. She had to have more... to make her cum.

Hissing back over her shoulder, she told him, "God damn it... do something more! Shove your finger in my behind!"

"Okay... baby! Here goes!" MacKay grunted, and without preparation, he searched out the tiny, crinkly-fleshed opening in the crevice of her slaving buttocks, shoving his middle finger deep into the warm sponginess of her rear passage.

Zoe groaned aloud. "That's it!" Instinctively, she writhed away from it... but as the pleasure-pain of it enhanced the ecstasy of her coupling, she screwed her hips back at him. "Come on, now... and fuck me hard!" she demanded.

MacKay jackhammered his cock into her wet, sloshing cunt with wild excitement, feeling the bulge of his finger in her anus through the thin separating membrane.

Then, suddenly, Zoe came, her body convulsing in orgasmic rapture. *"I'm cum-mmmiiiiiinnnnnnng!"* she screamed. *"Ahhhhhhh!"*

Dipstick grunted, as he pounded away behind her; then as he felt the slight burning of impending ejaculation, he jerked his finger from her rectum and drove even deeper and harder into her wildly clasping vagina... until his big cock erupted in a geyser of spewing semen. *"Christ!"* he moaned. "What a fucking ride... that was!" They collapsed together across the foot of the bed, Zoe sliding down to her stomach with Dipstick on top of her. He smiled to himself. Everything's working out, perfect! But he had to work fast now!

Hunter heard Zoe's scream as she came to climax with Dipstick MacKay. That bastard's ruined my plans for her – but good! I'll feed him his fucking cock... before I kill him!

In a very few moments, Dipstick got up off of Zoe, gave her behind a little pat and, stealthily, crept off the bunk bed. He dressed himself, quickly, then collected all of the gang's abandoned weapons. He had three pistols and three switch blade knives. The knives went into his pocket; the pistols were stuck in his belt. Every person in the trailer was busily engaged in a sex activity, except Gavin Rust. He raised up to see what Dipstick was doing... why he was fully dressed. Crawling off the bed, he approached MacKay, asking, "Where the fuck you going, man?" Only when Dipstick turned toward him did the small, bandy-legged, ferret-eyed gang member see the arsenal of weapons in Dipstick's belt.

It was too late. Dipstick drew one of the pistols and swung it in a short arc to crash against Gavin's forehead. The injured man went down, without a sound, sprawling heavily to the floor, unconscious.

Dipstick's next move was unpredictable. He gathered up Billie's clothing, then grasping her by her long, auburn hair, he pulled her mouth off of Dave's big jerking cock. "We're splitting!" he hissed at her. Get your ass off that square and let's go!"

"What the fuck are you talking about?" she asked. "W-We can't do that... and besides I'm going to cum... pretty soon!"

"To hell with that! I'm taking care of all that from now on! You're riding with me! You're going to be my mama!"

"Why... what's happening?"

"This's the end of Mitchell's rope!" he told her showing her the pistols.

Artie understood, instantly, as he listened to Dipstick. "Just cut us loose... and leave a couple of those guns!" he suggested.

"I'm not making it that easy!" MacKay grunted.

Dave looked down the length of the trailer to see that Hunter was slamming his cock, pile-drive hard, into his wife's demanding cunt... while the other, silvery-blonde gang member was forcing his prick deep into Lauren' mouth and throat. Zoe was stretched out at the foot of the bed... and in the middle of the floor Gavin Rust lay unconscious. God damn! He raged to himself. Both those sons-

Highway to Shame 215

of-bitches... are raping her at the same time! His cock jerked with frustration. Billie's mouth had brought him to the point of no return. Christ! His balls ached, terribly, with his need to cum. There was one thing Dipstick could do. He suggested it.

"Do one thing... before you go! Tell Zoe to come over here!"

"Okay!" He thrust Billie's clothes at her. "Start getting dressed!" He walked to the other end of the trailer, leaned over Zoe and murmured, "Go get into the other bunk, now... because all hell's going to bust loose in here... in just a few minutes!"

Zoe, sensing a favorable turn of events but not knowing exactly what was happening, obeyed. She got off the bunk bed, quietly, and padded to the other end of the trailer, suppressing a gasp as she saw Gavin Rust stretched out, still dead to the world. She sat down on the edge of the bed and waited.

Slipping on her jeans and shirt and carrying her jacket and boots, Billie Grant followed Dipstick MacKay out of the trailer. They ran to the gang's campsite, where MacKay rapidly stripped ignition parts from the other's motorcycles and flung them into the brush. In a few minutes, Billie was packed. He tied the pack onto his motorcycle and, with Billie up behind him, eased out of the campground. Always the opportunist, Billie had no qualms about what she was doing. All she knew was that she was riding with the smartest and the strongest. It was obvious that Hunter Mitchell was headed for a fall. Somewhere, she reasoned, he'd really screwed up.

The three people on the bed, at the rear of the trailer, were completely oblivious of all else but the rapture of their sexual couplings. Lauren, lay on her back while Hunter's cock thundered into her needful cunt, while at the same time, Frank Superini, his eyes closed, raced his long thin cock in and out of her warmly moist, sucking mouth. He was almost ready to cum. His breath was raspy and his hips jerked with the urgency of his need.

Without warning, the head of his cock began to expand, hotly, in her mouth. It was her first inkling of his nearness to orgasm. She hadn't even thought about it... before, until her mouth and throat was flooded with an almost continuous jetting flow of his white, hot, lewdly pumping semen. *Urghh! He's cumming, he's shooting his disgusting stuff i-in my m-mouth!* She swallowed... had to swallow to keep from gagging, while he used the strength of his legs to force it ever deeper into her throat. She heard his gasp of joy... and she kept sucking and swallowing, wildly... now suddenly wanting all of the biker's thick load... after her first shock of gagging revulsion.

Then, within a very few plundering strokes, Hunter, too, came to his thundering climax. His sperm shot from the slitted head of his demanding cock far up into the wildly clasping confines of her eager cunt.

"Christ!" he sighed contentedly. "Now that's what I call nice pussy!"

With a satisfied grunt he collapsed, twisting his body aside, slightly, because Frank Superini still sat astride her breasts, his cock rammed deep into her mouth, as the last of his cum was pumped from him.

It had taken only a few moments for Zoe to free Dave Christie and her husband, Artie; then, using the rolls of surgical tape, she knelt on the floor of the trailer and bound the unconscious Gavin Rust.

Artie slipped his P-38 Luger from a drawer, while Dave moved stealthily to the kitchen area where he found a ten-inch butcher's knife.

It was a surprised Frank Superini, who opened his glazed eyes to look into the muzzle of Artie's unwavering pistol. Berman, his face set in grim lines, warned him to silence and waved him off the bed. Dave and Zoe, working together, swiftly, tied him and gagged him. He lay on the floor of the trailer near Gavin Rust, his pale blue eyes blazing with helpless frustration.

What she was seeing didn't register on Lauren. She tottered on the crumbling edge of orgasmic release. Hunter had satisfied his own lust... and now he lay, heavily, on top of her, not moving, his cock growing flaccid within her inflamed vagina. She moaned aloud. "Oh, God... don't stop... now! Keep it up! Keep on f-fucking me... until I cum!"

Dave heard his wife's pleading. Damn... she's begging him for it... and the son-of-a-bitch can't do anything for her! The knowledge of her need... the fact she had begged to be fucked worked in him. He, too, had been brought to a towering level of desire... until Dipstick MacKay had pulled Billie's mouth off of him. Christ! He wanted to fuck his wife right away... but first he and Artie would have to immobilize the bearded bike gang leader!

Moving in close, holding the big knife in one hand, Dave reached out with the other, grabbed a large handful of Hunter's black hair and yanked his head up to glare into his face. Artie pressed the muzzle of his pistol against Mitchell's temple.

"Get up... slow and easy! It's all over... for you!" Dave growled.

Hunter was startled. "What the hell!" He tried to roll away, but Dave held him close, bringing the sharp butcher's knife up under his bearded chin until it pricked him deeply enough for the blood to flow.

"Move!" Artie Berman barked.

"Dipstick! Gavin! Superboy!"

"They can't help you. And one of your loyal gang split, taking your girl with him!" Dave laughed, jerking hard on Hunter's hair.

"Dipstick! It must've been Dipstick! I'll fucking *kill* him," Hunter roared, almost hysterically.

In a few seconds, he joined his companions on the floor of the trailer, trussed up and gagged securely.

On the bed, Lauren moaned aloud, "Oh, God... what's happening?" She was still in the throes of passion, needing and wanting a cock in her to bring her to the orgasm that was just beyond her reach. "P-Please... Dave... Artie... anybody? I-I want to cum! Oh, God... somebody... fuck me!"

Both Dave and Artie leaped to their feet and made for the bed. They reached it at the same time. "Hold off!" Dave warned. "She's my wife – and by God – I'm going to fuck her like she wants!"

"We can both fuck her!" Artie grunted. "No sweat!"

"How, goddamn it?"

"Easy! You take her in the cunt – and I'll take her in the ass!"

"Oh, *please*... don't talk – just *hurry!*" Lauren moaned, her hands clawing at her wildly needful pussy.

The husbands put down their weapons and climbed onto the bed.

Highway to Shame

"Turn her over on her belly!" Artie directed.

Numb to everything but the demanding need gnawing at the core of her being, Lauren was compliant in their hands, not caring, now, as she felt secure in the knowledge that Dave and Artie were there.

Quickly, Artie straddled her, a hand on each of the rounded cheeks of her quivering buttocks. With firm force he pulled them apart to reveal the tiny, puckered opening of her anus. Dipping the head of his cock, momentarily, into the copious liquids that virtually poured from her soaking cuntal gash, he directed it against the rubbery flesh of her rear passage.

And as Dave watched in astonishment, he forced it into the warm sponginess of her backside.

Lauren moaned with the pain of it... and Artie crooned to her, "Don't worry, Lauren, baby... you'll crawl the walls in a minute or two!" He drove it into her another inch. This time she screamed.

"Stop it, Artie! You'll split her apart!" Dave bellowed.

Zoe was there, now. Calmly, she said, "No... it won't! It'll hurt only for a moment or two! I should know!"

Then, with a final prodigious plunge, Artie gored his cock to the root of it, deep in her rear passage... and now she only moaned.

It was changing for her... as she adjusted to the unnatural presence. Tentatively, her hips ground in a tiny circle under him... around and around the rock-hard shaft of his cock buried in the buttery depths of her rectum.

Artie Berman dropped his full weight down on top of Dave's wife, then rolled swiftly to his side, his brawny arms wrapped around her to take her over with him, lightly as a feather. Instantly, Dave came between Lauren' legs. Guiding his expectant cock, that throbbed achingly from delayed action, straight into her, he plunged it to the hilt in one smooth stroke.

His wife moaned up into his face, "Fuck me... hard... now... damn it!"

He did.

And, under her, Artie sawed up into the clasping sheath of her rectum... as above with equal energy Dave plundered the receptive flesh of her cunt.

Under the double pounding of their cocks, as the two virile men fucked her, she soon began to spiral toward the orgasm that eluded her... and within a few minutes she convulsed between them, her release washing over her with emotional rapture. Never had she known anything like it, especially after the acute discomfort of her stretched anal passage had turned to ecstasy.

Then... she was there... and she shrieked out her pleasure.

"Oooooooooohhhhhh! It's here! I'm cumming! Oh! Oh! Ahh! Aaaaaaaaaaauuuuuuggggghh!"

She went limp, completely relaxed, like a rag doll between them, her senses swimming on the edge of unconsciousness. She saw, heard, smelled... but mostly, she felt! Oh, God! It feels... so absolutely... wonderful!

Zoe, watching, was stimulated, again and she wanted it too! She saw Lauren cum to her soaring orgasm and realized that neither of the two men had ejaculated.

Suddenly, she knew. She could... she would be able to have them... both of them!

"Artie! Dave! She's already cum!" she trilled. "Let me take her place! I want you both... to, fuck me!"

Dave heard her. "God damn! She's right! We can't do anymore for Lauren!"

He pulled rampaging cock from his wife's satiated cunt, and as Zoe Berman waggled her buttocks back at him, he knee-walked over to her. Reaching back, she guide his massive, hardened cock right into her anal passage. She helped him, pushing her hips back and rotating them, to ease his entrance.

Dave gasped, as his cock sunk into the clasping warmth of her backside, then following Artie's example, he turned Artie's wife over.

Finally, Artie was aware of what was

happening. He rolled Lauren from him and quickly mounted his wife.

When it was over, they rested, Artie served fresh drinks, and as they drank, they surveyed their three captives, not knowing yet what they should do with them.

"Let's finish our drinks first," Artie said. "I don't think they'll be going anywhere... yet!"

"I think we should just turn them loose!" Zoe suggested. "They'd certainly never try the same thing... with us... again!"

CHAPTER EIGHT

The vacation was over. It was Saturday morning, Lauren bustled about with her Saturday morning cleaning chores around the house. Dave was out in the yard. He had been mowing the lawn, but now, she didn't hear the sputter of the little engine. Peeking out the window, Lauren saw Dave talking to the new redheaded neighbor, one half of the English couple that had just moved in next door, and who was looking on with studied female helplessness while Dave tinkered with the engine of her lawn mower. *Well... it looks like Dave's moving in on her! It'll be just a matter of time... now...* She was dreamy for a moment, as she remembered the tall goodlooking husband of the well-built redhead. His name was Michael Simpson, and he had jet-black hair, too...

Then, she remembered that other man... the one with the black beard... the one called Hunter. She was glad they had decided to let them go. In a brutal way... he had done something extraordinary for her. She had found her true sexuality... her own self... under him, as he had slammed his big cock, into her.

The rest of their vacation had been spent with the Bermans. It had opened up a new life for her and Dave. Now, they were talking about sex... and they were swinging every chance they got. *I think it's only a matter of time until Dave breaks down and we'll join that club we were invited to...*

Twenty minutes later, Dave came into the house, sweating and whistling a happy tune.

"Well?" Lauren demanded.

"It was easy as apple pie!" he told her cheerily. "Michael and Davina Simpson are coming over for a barbecue dinner with us... tonight!"

"I'd better get out to the supermarket right away, then!" She felt a rising excitement.

"And be sure to check the liquor supply!" Dave reminded her.

She came into her husband's arms, offering her lips and giving her loins a suggestive grind up against him.

"What about tonight?" she murmured. "I saw Michael's cock when we met them for the first time the other day. Either it was huge or he had a whole Italian salami sausage stuffed into his pants."

"We'll just have to play it by ear... I guess: just make sure that both bedrooms are ready!" Dave directed. "And, if you don't stop that – you'll be getting it right here on the kitchen floor!"

"What's so bad about that?"

"It'd be great... except it might slow things down... tonight!" He used both hands grasping her rounded buttocks to pull her undulating loins in close to his awakening penis that had begun to throb to erection inside his pants.

"Okay... darling..." she agreed, writhing from his grasp.

"Come back here... you little prickteaser!"

"No... not now, Dave!" she smiled, picking up her car keys. "I've got things to do... to get ready for tonight... and we don't want anything to interfere with that... do we?"

THE END

Become an *Erotic*

IT'S NEVER BEEN EASIER TO SUBSCRIBE TO ONE OF THE MOST ORIGINAL MAGAZINES IN THE WORLD

ER appears 10 times a year
with 2 double issues.
For readers in the UK,
a year of literate smut,
delivered to your door,
costs only £25
(that's a 20% saving on the cover price)

- **10 issues**
- **1 year**
- **£25**

you can order by post to:

EPS, 54 New Street

Worcester WR1 2DL

Psst! Why not call and ask about our fabulous 'Try us for a pound' deal?
0800 026 25 24 (UK only)

Review Subscriber

Payment is simple – by credit card or cheque
Internet:
www.eroticreviewmagazine.com
Our friendly, free orderline:
0800 026 25 24
Subscribe by email:
leadline@eroticprints.org

JESSICA RODER

THROUGH A GLASS DARKLY...
A PHOTOGRAPHIC JOURNEY OF SEXUAL DISCOVERY

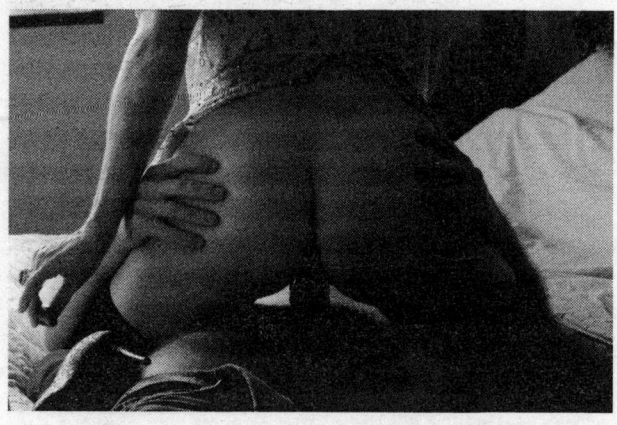

available from
ER BOOKS:
£14.95 plus p&p.
to order call
0800 026 25 24
or visit our website:
www.eroticprints.org

VITTORIA PERZAN
Trans/Sex

TAKE A WALK ON THE WILD SIDE:

ONE PHOTOGRAPHER'S VIEW OF THE WORLD OF TRANSEXUAL SEX

available from
ER BOOKS:
£14.95 plus p&p.
to order call
0800 026 25 24
or visit our website:
www.eroticprints.org

EROTIC REVIEW BOOKS

Erich von Götha's
THE TROUBLES OF JANICE
part 4:
Voyage to Venice

68 pp 297x210mm, colour
paperback - adult comic

£14.99
available from
ER BOOKS:

£14.99 plus p&p.
to order call
0800 026 25 24
or visit our website:
www.eroticprints.org

The Young Governess in Egypt
The sequel to the best-selling *The Young Governess*, by Phoebe Gardener. Upon the death of her lover, the eponymous heroine decides to visit Egypt, accompanied by her bi-sexual companion, Ruth. There a whole series of wild sexual adventures await them, including an erotic journey up th Nile, capture by Bedouin slave traders, and a magical stay in a rich man's harem.

Shameful Duties
Mary and Jessica Douglas, an attractive Chinese mother-and-daughter team desperately seek financial security. And they're prepared to get it, at almost any price. So when Victor Jordan, Fairview's richest man, courts Jessie, Mom is thrilled. However, the worst sort of sexual degradation awaits them both.

Havana Harlot
The daughter of millionaire businessman, Charlie, gets kidnapped on a family holiday in Cuba. In an attempt to defy the kidnappers, Charlie unintentionally causes his whole family to become the sexual playthings of the gang and they are forced to perform acts of unspeakable depravity with one another.

To order these PAST VENUS PRESS and any other titles:

Orderline: 0800 026 25 24
Email: leadline@eroticprints.org
Post: EPS, 54 New Street, Worcester WR1 2DL

*E*RB

WWW.EROTICPRINTS.ORG

THE BANKER'S WIFE
John Barbour

Funny how an innocent encounter can turn people's lives upside-down. When Artie and Diane Laurence 'clicked' with Max and Penny Byron at the year's dullest cocktail party, it might have gone no further than improving a potentially ghastly evening for these attractive couples. But the sexually sophisticated Byrons like to swing, and once they'd targeted the innocent young Laurences, the banker and his wife won't rest until they've scored – big time. Moreover, the banker's bisexual wife wants to play with both husband *and* wife. Penny is a beautiful, dangerous woman, just as predatory as her affluent, randy husband, while Diane Laurence's almost virginal naiveté and her husband's lack of experience leaves her totally exposed to this older couple's fiendish machinations.

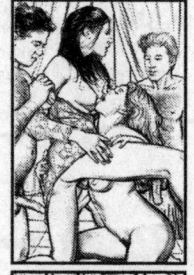

Orderline: 0800 026 25 24
Email: leadline@eroticprints.org
Post: EPS, 54 New Street, Worcester WR1 2DL

*E*RB

WWW.EROTICPRINTS.ORG

THE RAVISHED AMERICAN BRIDE
Bob Stainer

When Edward Tremayne brings Molly, his pretty new American bride, back to Cornwall, he warns her that his folks are not quite like others. Indeed, she is not expecting Firethorn, a large, imposing period house crammed to the eves with her delightful adult in-laws. Young Molly soon falls victim to the charm of her handsome father-in-law Piers, and his wife, Georgina, who looks almost the same age as their teenage children. But on the very first night of her stay she discovers a family secret that pulls her down into a spiral of decadent lust and depravity...

With oral, anal, and lesbian action, group incest, orgies and non-stop sex, this is a superb erotic tale in the setting of the lush English countryside. With exquisite illustrations by Tom Sargent.

Orderline: 0800 026 25 24
Email: leadline@eroticprints.org
Post: EPS, 54 New Street, Worcester WR1 2DL

WWW.EROTICPRINTS.ORG

ACADEMY OF LUST
Jenny Strong

Emily and Olivia Newbridge are heirs to a fabulously wealthy business empire that, one day, 22-year-old Emily is determined to run. Both sisters lack social skills, so their guardians send 18-year-old Olivia to a Swiss finishing school while Emily's employers invite her to a weekend seminar. Shockingly, both sisters are subjected to every sadistic torment and humiliation in the book! In their separate punishment worlds, they are forced to experience corporal punishment, public defloration, and many appalling perversions. But their bondage hells become submissive heavens and they gradually learn how to enjoy sex – on their own terms...

Featuring corporal punishment, bondage, defloration, urination and non-consensual sex, *Academy of Lust* suits a sophisticated erotic taste and is a superb BDSM read.

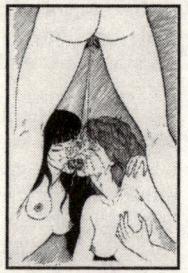

Orderline: 0800 026 25 24
Email: leadline@eroticprints.org
Post: EPS, 54 New Street, Worcester WR1 2DL

Call and ask about our great Past Venus Press 'Multiple Buy' deals! All Past Venus Press paperbacks are priced at £7.50 plus p&p, but our friendly staff are available to advise you about the best savings you can make with a multiple purchase, as a Gold Club member – or both!

Call 0800 026 25 24 (UK only) to find out more or visit our website at

www.eroticprints.org